HARD TRUTHS

ALEX WHITEHALL

RIPTIDE
PUBLISHING

Riptide Publishing
PO Box 1537
Burnsville, NC 28714
www.riptidepublishing.com

Hard Truths
Copyright © 2018 by Alex Whitehall

Cover art: L.C. Chase, lcchase.com/design.htm
Editor: Carole-ann Galloway
Layout: L.C. Chase, lcchase.com/design.htm

ISBN: 978-1-62649-847-1

First edition
October, 2018

Also available in ebook:
ISBN: 978-1-62649-846-4

HARD TRUTHS

ALEX WHITEHALL

RIPTIDE
PUBLISHING

To my families.

TABLE OF
CONTENTS

CHAPTER ONE

At the time, I didn't know that the hulking six-foot-four-inch tattooed biker wasn't actually dating my sister. They were certainly being handsy enough with each other.

Handsy at our parents' house, on Christmas Day. I stood to the side, studying my prim sister in her jeans and festive red sweater, wearing little jingle bell earrings and her hair all done up, and wondered if this was a dream.

He loomed above my five-eleven height and filled the entryway with broad shoulders and arms that could individually have picked me up. They were tattooed from his knuckles up to where they disappeared under his short-sleeved shirt, and more tattoos peeked out from the neckline of his shirt when he handed me his coat. The shirt, I should mention, was a plain black tee, snug against his bulging muscles. His hair was dark and short. Like, I'm-growing-it-out-from-shaved short.

When Sue—that's my sister—introduced him to the family, he smiled warmly and held out his hand to shake mine with a firm, confident grip, then pulled my dad into a bro-hug and called him "Pops."

My dad turned a funny color and mumbled what sounded less like a greeting than an insult.

Mom looked torn between being ecstatic that Sue had brought someone and horrified at the resulting date. She welcomed him into her house nonetheless, and he kicked off his boots before she had to ask. Maybe he'd seen the pile of shoes by the door—Dad and I never did get the hang of using the shoe rack—or maybe he wanted to show off his holey socks. They *were* very festive. Green, with reindeer who were obviously offering up some tail.

Unfortunately—fortunately?—my parents didn't seem to notice. I, on the other hand, had to fight a smirk to keep them ignorant. I did not want to be the one to explain to my mom why I found those cute lil reindeer funny.

The toes of one sock wiggled, and my eyes went up—and up—over the tight squeeze of the jeans across his muscular thighs and then along his rippling torso to meet his brown eyes. They crinkled in the corners when he smiled, and I smiled back, still in shock but also enchanted.

He winked.

Before my brain could process *that*—and the responding flutter that it sent through my body—Mom whisked everyone into the living room. I followed them in, definitely contemplating where this specimen of loveliness had come from and *not* staring at his ass.

See, he hadn't been at Thanksgiving, when Mom had heckled Sue and me that we were nearing our thirties, so we needed to settle down and get married and have lots of kids for her to dote upon and spoil. Sue and I had shared looks, wondering why her grandkids would get either of those when her own kids definitely hadn't. But we didn't say anything. That was one thing we'd both learned quickly as kids: shut the fuck up.

Dad didn't harp about the grandkids—he probably didn't want the goddamn nuisances running around when he'd just gotten rid of his own—but he had complained that we never visited, I never helped him fix up the house, and Sue had, god forbid, gotten a second set of piercings in her ears. Thankfully once he got food and booze in him, he mostly watched football, by which I mean slept on the couch. Whatever, one less parent to deal with.

Three days *after* Thanksgiving, Mom and I received a text from Sue: *I wanted to let you know I'll be bringing my boyfriend to Christmas dinner. Didn't want to rush him there for Thanksgiving, but we talked and xmas is good to go!*

This had been a surprise, since I hadn't known she was dating someone. And we weren't hellishly close or anything, but if she was dating someone seriously enough to bring to Christmas dinner, then she should have told her big brother.

Having seen him, it all made sense: she was embarrassed of him. Or of us. It was a fifty-fifty on which it was, but he obviously came from a very different world than the one we lived in. For comparison's sake, I should mention that while I was wearing jeans, like him, mine didn't have holes, and I had on a button-down. My own hair was trimmed conservatively—longer on the top, buzzed along the sides—and combed to the side for today. I had no visible tattoos or piercings, while he had a bridge, lip, and ear piercing.

Oh, and I was white. He . . . wasn't. At least he didn't appear white. Not white enough for my white-bread parents. Not that they'd say anything to his olive-toned face.

"So, what work do you do, Logan?" my dad asked with an edge to his voice, like he was hoping to embarrass him.

"Oh, freelance." Logan paused, then smirked. "You know, when I've got the time. This one keeps me busy."

He smacked my sister's ass and she giggled. The image was burned into my memory, despite my best attempts to scrub it away.

My father grunted. "What kind of freelancing do you do?"

"Whatever needs done. I've worked in warehouses, helped fill out security teams. Jobs where they're hiring for brawn." His eyebrows rose. "You ain't hirin', are you?"

"No! No. Nothing of the sort." Could Logan hear the disgust in his voice?

"Oh. Too bad." Obviously not. Logan shrugged, and his gaze slid to me. "What work do you do?"

My dick didn't know if it was going to be set on fire or shrivel from the gleam in his eyes, which seemed fifty percent *Go ahead, try to impress me* and fifty percent *I bet I could pin you against the wall with only one arm.*

Okay, that last one might have been my imagination. My very active imagination. Oh shit, there'd been a question. "I design websites."

His eyes went from challenging striptease to sparkling interest in a second flat, but quickly dimmed to indifference. Had I imagined it? "Oh. That must earn you bank."

"I do well enough." I shrugged, fighting down the heat that his gaze flared to life on my skin. "It's a fairly competitive field with a lot of fresh blood coming in, so I have to work hard to stay current and keep my job, and sometimes the hours can be grueling. But I love the work." Was I babbling? No one wanted to hear that much about my job. "So how'd you two meet?"

Logan swung an arm around my sister's shoulders, and she giggled again. I'd never seen her giggle so much. That was a good thing if it meant she was happy.

"Well," Logan said, pausing only briefly to nuzzle against Sue's neck and set off a fresh set of giggles, "I saw her profile on one of those dating sites and I messaged her and it was love at first contact." He chuckled lewdly, and it took me a moment to get what he was saying. I'd need to drink a lot tonight to scrub that thought from my mind as well. "It grew from there."

"So you met online," my dad said, his nose scrunching with distaste.

"Yeah, that's how everyone meets these days, Dad," Sue said, tilting her head onto Logan's shoulder and smiling widely. "How else was I going to meet someone like Logan?"

Dad would probably have said she shouldn't be meeting someone like Logan, but Mom announced that dinner was ready. Thank fuck.

Or I thought I should be thankful. Wrong holiday though.

"Would you like some green beans, Logan?" my mom asked him, offering the casserole up.

"Thanks, Mom, but I prefer meat."

Was I the only one who saw him flash that grin at me? Was I imagining it? Was he *flirting* with me in front of my sister and family?

"Oh," my mom said. "Well, there's plenty of turkey."

"I'm sure enough to fill me up."

Okay, I didn't expect my parents to get that reference, but certainly Sue—I glanced at her, but she was grinning like a fool as she piled mashed potatoes on her plate—or not. Maybe it was all in my head. Especially since Logan was putting helpings of peas, stuffing, and both sorts of potatoes on his plate. He obviously ate more than meat.

Then why had he said he preferred meat?

You know what? Whatever. He was my sister's boyfriend. If he wanted to make tasteless, stupid jokes in front of my parents, that was fine. She didn't seem bothered by it.

I tried to ignore him, but it was hard with him sitting directly across from me at the table. He had hellishly long legs, and his feet kept bumping mine. My legs were long enough that I couldn't tuck them under my own seat, so it was just something we had to deal with.

Least his presence meant I also didn't have to deal with my mom pressuring Sue and me to bring significant others to family events. She wasn't going to tell Sue to bring someone else, and after Logan, she likely wouldn't rush me into anything either. Not that I thought Logan didn't have a shot. They'd warm to him. Probably. They lived in a closed-off little world, but they weren't bad people. Or rather, I liked to think they weren't.

But maybe if I believed that, I would have told them I was gay. As it was, I didn't have any plans to tell them until I had a good reason to rock the boat and earn their potential ire. That reason would be a boyfriend who lasted long enough to be dragged to one of these gatherings. Hopefully someone as attractive as Logan, or else my sister would forever rub it in my face that she had better luck with guys.

I was drawn back into reality by Logan's foot bumping mine. Again.

"Yeah, so then I told the mofo—sorry, um, asshole—where he could stick it," Logan said, wrapping up a story I'd obviously missed.

"Oh. That's. That's . . ." My mom couldn't seem to finish.

"A stupid way to handle it. Why not call the police?" my dad asked, as if he knew the answer.

"Naw, the po-po would have thrown me back in jail, man."

Dad huffed derisively, shook his head, and returned his gaze to his plate.

Silence loomed across the table.

I took another bite of food. I wasn't even sure what it was. "Mom, the turkey turned out great this year. Not dry at all. Did you do something different?"

And yes, insulting my mother's cooking probably wasn't the best line of conversation, but I'd panicked.

Mom huffed. "I did the exact same thing I do every year, but this time I didn't buy a turkey full of antibiotics and chemicals and whatever else they load them with, so that must be why it turned out so well. I always knew all those drugs in the meat couldn't be good for us."

And yet she hadn't seemed to mind feeding it to us for the last twenty-some-odd years.

"Mom, I don't think those chemicals affect the moistness of the turkey," Sue chimed in.

"Well, I've done it the same every year and this year it's better, so I don't know what to tell you."

"Cheers." I raised my glass and took a drink before anyone joined me. Logan downed a good half of his wineglass, and Sue seemed to be smirking behind her glass of water.

I really needed to have a talk with her alone today.

It didn't seem likely that I would get a chance, though. Logan was glued to her hip—not that I could blame him. I wouldn't want to be left alone with my family either. When she and I volunteered to clean up, Logan followed us into the kitchen. My sister insisted a guest shouldn't be put to work, so he leaned against the counter watching us. I could feel his gaze prickling the back of my neck as Sue and I washed, rinsed, and dried.

"So," I said, "how long have you two been dating?"

"Oh god, Isaac, not the third degree from you too?"

I sighed. "Sorry for making conversation."

"In that case, when are you going to bring a little wifey home?"

Behind us, Logan snorted what sounded like a chuckle.

"Shove it," I grumbled.

"Exactly. How about you tell me more stories about that client from hell with the president who changed his mind every time you gave him updates?"

Yeah, bitching about work was the easiest thing to do, and I was glad to, especially if it meant not talking about my nonexistent love life and my super-nonexistent straight love life. Not to mention I had enough stories about this particular client that I could have filled the entire cleaning-up time with them. Actually, I probably could have filled the entire day with stories of this asshole—may he never hire my company again, please—but I wasn't that self-centered. I gave a few of the best ones, then asked about her business. She'd opened one of those yoga/women's fitness/massage studios and was always complaining about not having enough customers and how WASPish the ones she had were. I got the impression she enjoyed the complaining, because she *glowed* whenever she talked about her baby.

So we chatted about nothing in particular and definitely nothing important with Logan lurking over our shoulders—and my sister's obvious desire not to talk about him. Then the dishes were put away.

We all tromped back into the living room—and woke Dad up— to exchange presents.

Can I say that it's kinda awkward to buy a present for someone you've never met? But you can't *not* get a gift for your sister's boyfriend at Christmas when he's going to be sitting there. We all piled onto the sofas—Logan and Sue on the love seat; Mom, Dad, and I on the couch—then Mom leaped to her feet and began handing out the presents under the tree while Sue and I moved as little as possible from our spots to hand out the gifts we'd brought.

To his credit, Logan looked surprised to be getting gifts. And damn, his smile of instantaneous joy was gorgeous. Wide, pearly whites flashing, skin glowing. "Thank you," he said when my mom handed him two little boxes, one of which I would bet was a gift card tied around something heavy.

Then I handed him what I'd gotten, and his eyebrow quirked a bit more playfully. "Thank you. This is unexpected."

I tried to just smile, sit back on the couch, and not get lost in those eyes. I hadn't noticed before, but his eyes were stormy gray rather than brown. Quite fetching. Plus the crinkles at the corners were still as alluring as they'd been on first meeting him— And I needed to stop staring at *my sister's boyfriend*. I pulled my small pile of presents onto my lap, sorting through the ones wrapped with perfection and the two from Sue in gift bags because she and I shared the inability to wrap anything that wasn't a book or a DVD. It made it super obvious when we were or weren't giving the other one of those things.

She had two wrapped gifts and a bag from me this year. She grinned as she picked up one of the totally-a-DVD's and shook it like a little kid. "I wonder what this could be?"

"It's actually a gift card in an empty DVD case that I'll need back, so the joke's on you!"

"Hah! I'm totally using that next year."

Finally my mom finished handing out presents and returned to her seat, and we—as we did every year—each opened a gift from youngest to oldest before it became a free-for-all. As excited as I was to open my presents and watch my family open what I'd bought them, my eyes kept being drawn to Logan as he unwrapped what we'd gotten him. The first thing was a simple jewelry box with a gift card to Dunkin' Donuts, and the second was a box of hot chocolate mix with a Target gift card taped to it.

As silly as those gifts were, he smiled and said thank you. He did this thing when he seemed a little embarrassed, where he rubbed the top of his head. I wanted to joke that he'd go bald if he did that too often, but then it'd be obvious I had been staring, so instead I kept staring as he opened my gift.

Did I mention that it's really hard to buy a present for someone you've never met, especially when your beloved sister's idea of helpful hints is *whatever* and *gift cards* and *he likes coffee*—which explained my parents' gifts to him.

Mine weren't much better. I'd gotten him a high-end bag of ground coffee that I loved—and saved for my weekend cups so I could truly savor it, because *damn* it was pricy—and a mug that had seemed like a good idea at the time, but with my parents sitting here watching, I was beginning to second-guess giving it to someone I didn't know.

He pulled the mug out of the bag, took a second to read it, then burst out laughing. When he'd finished, he glanced up at me and his grin was bright enough to burn my retinas. "Thanks, it's perfect. I love foxes."

Warmth flooded through my veins, and I was about ready to break out in a sweat.

"What is it?" my mom asked, and I prepared for the worst.

"It's a mug from Isaac." He held up the mug that read *For [image of a fox] sake*. "I don't know how he knew I liked foxes, but thanks."

My mom's brow scrunched, and I could see her struggling to figure out the mug. I hoped she never would. To that end, I distracted her by thanking her for the button-down she'd gotten me. It didn't matter that I only wore them at work or when visiting on the holidays—at least it meant I rarely had to go out and buy my own. She didn't believe in toys or fun things as presents now that we were adults.

My sister, on the other hand, had bought me an anime series called *Kids on the Slope*, which my mom would probably think was a children's show because it was animated. I was fine with her thinking that, or else she might start wondering about shows Sue'd gotten me previous years.

Finally all the presents were opened and shuffled out of the way. My dad settled in for his nap and turned the TV on, which cued my mom to invite the rest of us to the tiny kitchen table for a game of cards.

And that was when it happened.

I wasn't sure how we ended up there, but my mom and Sue were in the kitchen down the hall and around the corner. Coming back from the bathroom, I was passing Logan in what had suddenly become a narrow hallway. Well, his shoulders were really broad.

I stopped and turned sideways, back to the wall so we'd fit, and then he was standing in front of me, far closer than necessary, not touching me but not arm's-length away, and *damn* he was tall and *fit*.

And smiling in a way that was not sweet or innocent at all. "Thanks for the Christmas presents. I very much appreciate it."

He totally casually put out a hand against the wall, pinning me from continuing toward the kitchen.

I swallowed, and heat flooded my face and other places not my face. "Hey, sure. I mean, we—I want you to feel welcome if my sister's serious about you."

His chuckle was downright *dirty*, and I swore he leaned in a little closer. "Honestly? I liked the mug, and your sister's sweet, but I'd rather be unwrapping you this Christmas."

In case I hadn't gotten his implication—which I absolutely had— his hand touched my hip, slipped over my ass, gave a squeeze for good measure, and was gone just as quickly. Then I was alone in the hallway, not sure when he'd vanished, trying to get my racing heart under control.

Had that really happened? Had that really fucking happened? Sue's boyfriend had *hit on me*? In my parents' house. On Christmas. With my sister a stone's throw away. Oh god. I had to tell her. I had to let her know before they got any more serious. Maybe he was joking. Maybe it was a misunderstanding—although I wasn't sure how I could misinterpret his hand on my ass. Maybe they had an open relationship?

But how many relationships were open enough to involve one person fucking both siblings? I definitely didn't want to fuck a guy that was fucking my sister.

Well, I wanted to fuck the guy, but not if he was fucking my sister.

Christmas dinner was sitting like a lava lamp in my stomach.

I whipped out my phone and flipped to my sister's text thread. *Um, your boyfriend grabbed my ass.*

Probably not the most eloquent, but I was still standing in the hallway rubbing where his hand had been, and I might not have been getting enough blood to my brain to formulate coherent thoughts.

My phone pinged.

Did you like it? she replied.

Did you read what I fucking wrote? Your boyfriend hit on me! I hoped she could sense how hard I was hitting those digital keys.

Don't worry. I'll talk to you later about it. Come back and play cards. Mom is trying to both tell me to break up with Logan and to have a boyfriend, and it's painful.

I stared at her text long enough that Logan passed me in the hall again on his way back to the kitchen. He didn't stop and grope me—no, I wasn't disappointed—but moved along like nothing had happened.

And my sister was telling me not to worry about it. I was starting to question her relationship with Logan. Mostly in all caps as internet abbreviations, like WTF, WTH, and OMG.

I followed Logan to the kitchen and my family and the cards. The only open seat was the one across from him. I wanted to glare at Sue, as if this was her fault, but sat instead. A few seconds later, I realized his feet bumping into mine under the table earlier hadn't been an accident.

"So what game do you want to play?"

"Poker's the only one I'm familiar with," Logan said. Because of course. He winked. "And we could make it interesting."

"I, um, I'm not sure that's a good idea," my mom said, and I agreed.

Mostly because Strip Poker With Logan was the sole game on my mind, and that was so horribly inappropriate that the shock of my own thoughts was the only thing keeping my boner in check.

"Blackjack?" Logan suggested.

Sue laughed and bumped her shoulder against his. "Don't worry, we'll teach you Kings in the Corner."

What followed was a surprisingly tame, enjoyable game of Kings in the Corner. Logan cut back on lewd comments and shifted to fake betting, commenting on his homies, and making another reference to having been in prison.

My mom got quieter and quieter as the game continued.

I, on the other hand, kept studying Logan and Sue and was beginning to pick up on other things. Like how they weren't being nearly as handsy now. Had Sue taken my warning to heart and gotten mad at him? But no, she hadn't seemed concerned, and it wasn't like she was pushing away his advances. Instead, over the course of the hour, they'd shifted from disgustingly cute couple in love to two friends hanging out with family.

And then it dawned on me.

Between games, I escaped to the bathroom so I could text her. *Holy shit you brought a fake date to Christmas.*

Her response was delayed enough that I worried I'd have to leave the bathroom or else people would begin to suspect my intestines had exploded.

But finally: *I have *no* idea what you're talking about ;)*

Holy shit. My sister had brought a fake date to Christmas.

Which opened up a whole other set of questions.

Why? How did they meet? How did one go about finding a fake date for the holidays? HolidayHunkHunter.com? Why hadn't she told me about this?

Well, I reasoned, finishing up in the bathroom, *if she had told me, I'd have wanted to bring someone.* And that would have looked suspicious. Especially since I'd have brought a man, which would have opened more than a can of worms. Maybe it was best that she hadn't told me after all.

Back in the kitchen, I apologized for taking so long, but they'd given up on playing cards and were chatting while munching on cookies. Mom was mostly slaughtering a summary of a movie she'd seen—one I'd also seen but I wasn't going to mention that.

"I just don't see why they had to make him gay. It had nothing to do with the plot," she said at the end, a small frown sending a cascade of wrinkles down her chin.

"They didn't make him gay," Sue said before I could.

Not that I could have. My tongue seemed to have swollen and stuck to the roof of my mouth.

"He simply was gay," Sue continued. "That's like saying 'I wish they hadn't made him black.'"

"I didn't say that!" Mom complained. "And anyway, that's apples and oranges. It's not like he could help being black."

A little more of me shriveled inside. Logan's foot bumped against the instep of mine and didn't move. Neither did I.

Sue sighed. "Mom, people are born gay or not. It's not like dying your hair. He was gay in real life, so they made him gay in the movie."

"But why did they have to flaunt it? It had nothing to do with the story!"

"They didn't flaunt it," I finally managed. "They showed him with his boyfriend."

"Exactly! I don't want to see *that stuff* when I go to the movies."

Sue arched a brow. "Were there explicit sex scenes? Because I thought it was rated PG-13."

"They *kissed*." Mom sounded scandalized.

"People kiss in movies all the time!" Sue kept her voice calm, but her hands did all the shouting.

"But not *those* people!"

I fought hard not to wince, and Logan's foot rubbed against mine under the table, like a silent voice of support. Telling me he and my sister were both there for me. Well, the guy had groped me, so it only made sense. He'd better be on my side if he was . . . on my team.

Wow, that even sounded stupid in my head.

"Hey," Logan said before my sister could respond with what, based on her expression, was likely going to be a heated retort, "I thought you weren't supposed to talk politics at the table with guests."

He gave a friendly grin, as if he were a silly ol' man who didn't know etiquette, and Sue caught herself.

"You're right. Mom, we can talk about this later. Zacky—"

"Oh god, don't call me that."

"—you should tell Mom about that client who wanted everything in pink and purple with glitter accents."

So I did. It was a hilarious story—although it'd been endlessly frustrating at the time. It had ended up okay though: the client had realized that maybe there were benefits to not going overboard and that maybe her designers knew what they were talking about. We'd included all the *main* design features that she'd wanted without making the viewer want to stab themselves in the eyes. But the story got to be dramatic and over the top—exactly like the client had been.

Everyone was laughing by the end, although Logan and Sue had already heard me tell the story—and with more cursing. At least it had changed the subject. Shortly after, Dad was awake and itching for pie, so we shuffled into the dining room and moved on with our day, the horrors of men kissing on-screen forgotten.

That was the tricky part about being with family. It was easy to fall into the same patterns, to ignore what you didn't like about each other, to put up with each other, because there was a basis of love. Or enough of it that continuing to follow those patterns was easier than stopping would be. It was why Sue and I came even though we disagreed with a lot of our parents' thinking. It was why Mom and Dad didn't disown Sue even though they'd always threatened to if she was sexually active before marriage. It was why they held their tongues—for today—about how disappointed they were in her bringing Logan to our family Christmas. I'm sure she'd get an earful later over the phone, but for now we all played nice.

Which was how the day passed. Then it was time to go and we packed our cars with our presents. We all took turns hugging, giving me a chance to demand Sue explain everything to me later. I ended up getting a bear hug from Logan. Or it had seemed like it was going to be a bear hug, and from the outside it probably looked that way. From the inside, his groin was pressed against mine and he didn't mutter Christmas greetings but directions.

"Check your back pocket."

Then he released me and gave my parents the same great big hug—with less crotch contact, I hoped—and we piled into our cars and left.

I had survived another Christmas. This one had certainly been an adventure, and I had a two-hour drive home to think about it. Not that it helped. By the time I pulled up to the curb in front of my condo, I still hadn't figured much more out about Sue and Logan and all that had happened. Perturbed, I tried not to think about it anymore as I unloaded my car.

It was only when I took off the jeans and pulled on sweats that I remembered Logan's instructions. In my back pocket where he'd groped me, he had also slipped a business card with his name, contact information, and a web address, with *Call me!* scribbled across one edge.

I stared at the card for a good long while, part of my brain trying to come to terms with the fact that this had come from my sister's boyfriend—although most of me knew it had all been an act. Still, that wasn't something I wanted to deal with tonight. My sister had a farther drive than I did, and I was exhausted. I set the card on the kitchen table, grabbed my tablet, and slumped on the couch to get lost in a book.

Sue, Logan, and Christmas realizations could all wait until the next morning.

CHAPTER TWO

I woke up with a food hangover, my mouth dry and my head begging for caffeine. I fell out of bed, shivering as the chill air hit my skin, pulled on my sweats and hoodie, and stumbled into the kitchen, where I'd thought far enough ahead last night to set the timer, and a cup of coffee was brewing for me.

A true Christmas miracle. Along with not having work. Thank the powers that be for long weekends. I tossed a bagel into the toaster and slumped against the counter while I waited for everything to be ready.

My gaze landed on the business card I'd left carelessly on the table, the white exceptionally bright this morning in the natural light. Or else my caffeine needs were critical. Either way, I was reminded of Logan and Sue and yesterday, and I searched for my phone.

A text this morning from Sue: *Call when you're up.*

Command obeyed.

"Morning, Isaac!"

"Hey. You've got some explaining to do."

"Me? You're the one who couldn't keep his eyes off my boyfriend!" Her righteous indignation was so fake, I didn't need her laughter to clue me in.

I ignored what it meant that I'd been caught staring. "And that's the first thing you need to explain, missy!"

"Okay, okay. You're sick of Mom harassing us about not having dates too, yeah?" She didn't pause for me to answer. "So I was on this site and saw this dude offering up his services. Pretty much to be a date for someone to take to a holiday dinner. Good or bad, although you know which I wanted to shove in Mom's and Dad's faces. He was willing to be worse, but I said he could totally go low-key with it. Mom and Dad aren't bad, yeah? Only kind of . . . unexposed. So I thought it'd be good if they faced everything they feared and had to play nice. And Mom wasn't going to say anything with him there, so you and I would get out of it for a bit."

"And what did Logan—if that is his real name—get out of it?"

"He's got no family and his friends were going through a *thing* this year—I didn't ask for details—so he was gonna be alone for Christmas. Or maybe he wanted to avoid his friends' Christmas, I dunno. This way he got company and dinner. And a new friend, because he is *hilarious*. We went on fake dates so we'd actually know each other, and he's a blast!"

I scoffed. "Maybe you'll be dating him for real next year."

"Yeah, if he didn't bat for your team, that might be an option."

My throat closed and my stomach clenched. The silence between us stretched, tightening the noose around my neck as I struggled to breathe and speak.

"Sorry," Sue said, her voice softening. "I shouldn't assume. But, uh, I got the impression from some of your posts online that you were gay. And I probably should have said something. I'm sorry. I guess I wanted you to feel safe enough with me to tell me yourself, but that was kind of an asshole move. So, Isaac, I love you and it doesn't matter if you're gay. If you are, I want you to know that I'm a safe space."

"Thank you." It was the only thing I managed to squeak out. Probably because I was too busy wiping tears from my cheeks. I cleared my throat and tried again. "Thank you. That means a lot. And yeah, you're right, I'm gay." I paused, then added, hoping for levity, "For all the good it's done me getting a guy."

She giggled. "Well, Logan's gay, if that helps."

"Listen, just because we're both gay—"

"And you were eye-humping him the whole day."

"—doesn't mean we're Noah's fucking matched pair."

"I know. But he mentioned that you were hella cute."

I ignored the excited *thump* of my heart. "He actually said, 'hella cute'?"

"No, he said, 'Why didn't you tell me your brother was a hotter guy version of you?' Which made me almost crash the car, so I was trying not to relive it."

My bagel popped, and I nearly dropped the phone. "So. Yes. Um." I blamed my inability to form a sentence on the fact that I was trying to talk and butter a bagel and I still hadn't had a cup of coffee yet.

"That's what I thought. I mean, I've got eyes. Logan is hella cute too. And you can't deny you were interested."

"He gave me his card. Business card?" I said by way of answering.

"Then call him. If you want." She said that last part as if giving me a way out. Wasn't that nice of her?

"Won't Mom and Dad be a little confused if I start dating your boyfriend?"

"Something tells me they'll be too distracted by the fact you're dating a guy to harp on the details."

And there was the awful truth. "I guess it wouldn't hurt to call."

"You should. And you two can totally geek out together over graphic resolutions and visual layouts. *Plus* he's already sister-approved!"

"Because that's definitely what I dig in a guy. My sister's approval." She snorted. "Maybe you should."

"I am not having this conversation before my first cup of coffee, so we need to change the subject." Speaking of—I poured a glorious mugful and added a teaspoon of sugar, then took cup and bagel to the table.

"That's all I've got. I figured it'd be better to have this talk on the phone. And I wanted to apologize for not telling you before, but I needed you to have a natural surprised reaction."

"To see if I was a bigoted racist too?"

"No, but you are shit at acting."

"I'm hanging up now."

"I love you!"

I chuckled. "I love you too, Sue. Thanks for calling to let me know the truth. I was kind of surprised when your boyfriend wanted to unwrap me."

"He what?"

"Talk to you later."

"No! Wait—"

I hung up. Then immediately texted her: *It was all good. He was slipping me his number.*

That might not have been the full truth, but she hadn't seemed upset with him hitting on me while they were "dating." After all, it *would* make him less desirable to Mom and Dad if they found out he was cheating on his girlfriend with her brother.

Which was too complicated a thought for this early in the morning. I took a long sip of coffee and sighed.

Yes, there was no rush. Now it was a matter of working up the nerve to contact Logan—if that was something I wanted to do.

Who was I kidding? Of course it was. Though maybe not before breakfast.

In fact, the day after Christmas probably wasn't ideal at all. But his *Call me!* didn't have many details, and the longer I waited, the more awkward it would become. So I ate my breakfast, fortified myself with coffee, took a shower, got dressed, and sat down to google him. Like a true nerd do.

I was surprised to find the website on the business card was for *his* graphic design business, which meant the *freelancing* that he'd mentioned was both true and false. I browsed the site, checking out work he'd done for previous clients and some of his avant-garde selections. He did good work, and if the company I worked for didn't already have a full staff of graphic designers, I would have nudged them toward him. As it was, I flipped through his site, appreciated his talent, and didn't nitpick about the site's construction.

Not that I based potential dates on their use of white space and intuitive navigation interface.

There wasn't much to find about him online—he seemed to be a private man. All his social media accounts were friends locked, so I could see that he had the accounts, but not what he did with them.

Which meant there was nothing left to do but call him.

After I went to pick up some groceries.

It wasn't because I was stalling—I just needed groceries. And it was rude to call someone you didn't know too early in the morning.

It didn't have to do with the fact that I had *no idea* what to say to him when I called. *Oh hey, so I hear you go on dates for the cost of a holiday dinner?*

Yeah. That would go over great. I tried to brainstorm something better while I shopped, then put the groceries away, then washed my dishes, then vacuumed, but I came up blank. The phone was in my hand, ringing through to his number, and I still didn't know what I was going to say.

I should have texted him instead.

"Hello?"

A warmth shuddered through my body. I hadn't remembered his voice being so deep and sultry before. It definitely hadn't had this effect on me yesterday, although the fact that I had been thinking of him as my sister's boyfriend had probably made me compartmentalize a little. Now it definitely was causing a reaction.

"Hello?" he said again, sounding less sultry and more confused.

"Hi." Said me, the most eloquent of all.

"Hi." He chuckled. "Who is this?"

"Isaac. Hi, this is Isaac, Sue's brother. You gave me your card yesterday. Assuming this is Logan?"

"Yeah, this is Logan." He paused, his voice warm again when he spoke. "I'm glad you called."

"Yeah. I, uh, didn't want to call too early. And I had to talk to my sister."

"So you know there's no risk of me being your future brother-in-law?"

"Thanks for making this creepy."

"Sorry." But I heard the smile wrapped around that word. "I'm glad you talked to her and cleared things up."

I shrugged and paced around the coffee table. "Some things, at least."

"Want to go out for drinks and clear up the rest?"

I snorted. "Presumptuous, aren't you?"

Amusement colored his words. "I figure you wouldn't call if you weren't at least a little interested. And your sister seems to like me, so I hope she gave a good recommendation—"

"She called you, didn't she?"

He outright laughed. I would dare call it a guffaw. "No, I swear she didn't. I'm merely hopeful."

"Okay."

"Okay?"

"Yeah. Drinks today sound good. Though, do you live down by her?"

"Same town as you, actually. She might have let that slip on the ride home."

I wasn't even the slightest bit upset with her. "You know Café Fin?"

"Yep. At four?"

I pulled my phone from my ear to glance at the time. It was only one. I hesitated. Three hours to absolutely not think about the totally not a date? "Um, can you make it any earlier?"

"Oooh, eager are we?"

I gave a wry look to my blank TV in place of him, hoping he could hear it in my voice. "Oh yes, oh baby, I need to see you."

"Well, when you put it that way . . . how about two?"

It was exactly what I'd asked for, and yet I hesitated, a hard knot in my stomach. Which was stupid. It was drinks. Not like it was Christmas dinner with the family. Humor bubbled up and out, escaping my lips on a chuckle. "Yeah, two works."

"Good, I'll see you then."

"See you then."

We hung up, and I glanced down at my clothes. Jeans and a ratty hoodie. Butterflies flooded around the rock in my gut. What a great first—second?—impression. I needed to change.

Maybe he liked the clean-cut boy I was at home—opposites attract and all that. If so, he was in for a bit of a surprise. Not that I cared. He had to like me as me, right?

Oh god, I was becoming a complete idiot over this. We were *going out for drinks*. Coffee and maybe pastries, not booze and a blowjob. I just needed to dress like I would with any of my friends and let the damn chips fall where they may. Logan obviously owned T-shirts and jeans, and he wouldn't care that I had tattoos and piercings. If he did? Fuck him.

My brain stuttered over that with an eager *Yes, please!* But I ignored it and pulled on dark-wash jeans, a green long-sleeved shirt with my favorite black *I do mass quantities of code* shirt over top, and a leather cuff. A touch of eyeliner—which I refused to call *guyliner*—and some gel in my hair. He still couldn't see my tattoo and piercings—although if I inhaled deeply and the shirt stretched taut against my chest, he could maybe figure one of them out—but I wasn't the button-down boy from the day before.

It felt good.

He could learn about the holey-hoodie-wearing side of me later if things went that direction.

Eventually I pulled on my peacoat and scarf, caught the bus, and arrived at the little café tucked on a strip of mom-and-pop shops. I pushed past the wreath-decorated door and was welcomed by the jingle of a bell, the heavenly aroma of coffee, and a half-filled seating area. A quick scan found Logan at a table already, a cup loosely held by his right hand, his phone in his left, although his eyes were on me. He smiled, inviting me over with nothing more than a twitch of his eyebrows. The same *zing* of attraction from yesterday shot through me—this time with the added benefit of not feeling weird. Although the draw to the counter to order a drink was strong, I made my way to the table he'd chosen against the far wall.

Today he was wearing a black button-down, showing a little of his chest tattoo and also a braided leather necklace with a silver pendant I couldn't make out—and certainly wasn't going to squint at like an idiot. The fit of the shirt emphasized his broad shoulders in a way that the tee the day before hadn't, and it did nothing to keep me from staring at them. I already felt the heat creeping up my neck as I stood by his table. "Hey."

"Hello." A long pause dragged out, and he chuckled awkwardly. "Um, want to get a drink first?"

"Yes. Sure. Be right back." As if there were a chance I would take the coffee and run.

"I'll be here." As if he would run while I wasn't watching. I guess if he didn't like the new me—the real me—he might have been tempted. But that smile he'd thrown hadn't seemed disappointed. At all. It had seemed . . . hungry.

"Do you want to split something?"

The faint lines of surprise on his face made the rough biker attitude shift straight into adorable—especially since he didn't have any of the piercings he'd had yesterday. "Like what?"

"A muffin? A croissant? A sausage quiche?"

"No, I'm good. I might be hungry later, though." Oh, that smile was a tease, promising things I wasn't nearly lucky enough to get, I was sure.

I managed to arrive at the service counter without tripping over anything, despite my mind being firmly planted in *What would you be hungry for later?* territory. I ordered my drink and returned to the table on autopilot. After setting my drink down, I unwrapped the scarf and slid the coat off, hanging them both on the back of my chair before I sat. I pulled my drink closer before I peeked up to him, worried about the silence, and found him staring, lips slightly parted.

The heat that had left my cheeks while I'd waited in line returned full force. "What?"

"Nothing." He cleared his throat. "Nothing, you look good."

Relief washed through me. "Thanks. I was worried you were expecting the same guy who was at my parents' house."

His eyebrow twitched. "You aren't him?"

I gestured at his shirt. "Clothes don't make the man, do they?"

Logan smiled. "I guess not. I should admit that I might have amped up my history—"

"And current job?"

"And that. For your parents."

"I figured. At least a little. And the piercings?"

"Fake. The maintenance for real ones seems like too much bother, but your sister thought it'd add to my appeal, so she rigged some fake ones."

"And you didn't mind playing up a stereotype?" I knew he was the one who'd put the ad in the whatever, but I found it hard to believe he'd been okay with walking into an environment where his brown skin would be instantly judged.

He shrugged. "I kind of liked it. Sorta like putting on a costume. The person they were judging wasn't the real me—even if they would have judged me too. Sue asked the same thing, and I have to admit, when I listed the ad, it was on a lark. I didn't expect anyone to take me up on it. But talking to her . . . Well, she seemed embarrassed to be thinking about doing it—"

"But she still did it."

Logan snorted a laugh. "Yeah. But we talked about it a lot. I guess if I'd had more problems growing up, I would have had an issue. But I'm Mexican and Italian, and just light enough to 'pass' most of the time." He rolled his eyes. "So it didn't bother me as much as maybe it should." His lips twisted momentarily. "And Sue being worried for my feelings helped."

I nodded, glad she'd made him feel comfortable in what could have been a pretty awful situation. "And thankfully the day went pretty well."

"Yep. The turkey was barely dry."

It was my turn to roll my eyes. "So what else was fake? I'm pleased to see the tattoos were real."

"Definitely. I am still the kid from the wrong side of the tracks."

I raised a brow. "I saw the address of your company. You're certainly on the 'right' side now. Also, you own a company. That's impressive."

"I don't think it counts when it's only me—it's freelancing."

"So what you told my dad wasn't a lie."

He smirked. "Exactly."

"Then you need to tell me about the real you."

"Uh-huh." He pointed to my hair and shirt. "And you need to tell me about the real you, it seems."

I sighed. "Fair enough. Mine's simple though: I'm pretty much who I am with my parents. But I curse more, listen to music they wouldn't approve of, fuck guys, and generally think differently than everything they'd want me to think."

"I'm liking the real you better already."

"Good. Not that there's anything wrong with the other me. My parents just haven't been exposed to much outside their world. Sue and I try to introduce new stuff, but they close down pretty fast. We only see each other at holidays, so it's easier to fit into the mold they remember about me."

"Even the hair?"

I shrugged. "My dad would probably tell me it 'looks gay' and it would all spill out from there."

"So no plans to tell them?" He asked it casually, but a hint of tension ran beneath the question, as if this was important to him.

"If I had a significant other who I wanted to take home? Yes, I'd tell them. But for now I don't see the need to rock the boat."

"Might give them a chance to come to terms with you being gay—bi?—before you throw a boyfriend in the mix."

"Gay. And . . . maybe. You've seen them. But they're my parents. I don't want to lose them if I don't have to." I stared down at my drink, uncomfortable with how intense the conversation had become. "You out to your parents?"

"I was." The depth of sadness in his voice drew my eyes to him.

I saw the firm line of his lips and remembered that Sue had said he didn't have any family. "I'm sorry."

"It's . . . Well, it is what it is." His gaze flickered down to his cup, then back up, and he mustered a smile. "They were great while I had them though. When I came out, my mom said she was grateful she wouldn't have to worry about me knocking some girl up. She was joking—I think. Mostly."

I tried not to sigh in envy. "She sounds great. I don't think my parents would ever joke about me knocking someone up." I scrunched my nose. "My mom might actually be happy about it. Think it would force me to settle down."

"Yeah? She thinks you'll step up and take responsibility?"

"I guess so. But if I was going to take responsibility, I'd take the kid and run from the woman."

Logan snickered. "Poor woman."

"Thankfully it's not going to be a problem." I paused. "Well, it's highly unlikely to be a problem. Won't be with a woman, at any rate."

"Let's hope no little babies appear unless you want them to."

Heat crept up past my jaw and into my cheeks. I'd gone on a bit of a ramble, hadn't I? About babies. About making babies. On a coffee date. Kill me now. "Yes. Right. So . . ." Oh god. Thoughts. I'd had thoughts a moment ago! I put my cup to my lips to stall for time, and traced back to our original conversation. "You were going to tell me which is the real you."

"A little bit of both. I don't normally wear a button-down for coffee, but I kind of wanted to impress you. I wear it when I'm dealing with clients—"

"Oh, so now I'm a client?"

"Hey now! I'm not that sort of freelancer." Logan paused while I got my snickers out. No, it wasn't that funny, but it tickled my funny bone. "I wanted you to see that I wasn't some bad-boy biker like what I showed your parents."

"But you *are* a bad-boy biker?"

He smirked. "I might have ridden my bike here."

"Nice." I tried not to leer too much.

"And I did a lot of odd jobs when I was younger—warehouse work, construction, anything to make money. But that was to pay for college and tattoos. Things got a little rough in high school—I might have hit that rebellion phase extra hard—but I've left most of that behind me. So now I'm the bad-boy biker who wears a suit sometimes."

That wasn't a problem in the least. I had visions of him riding his bike—it was a Harley in my mind, all black with gleaming silver—wearing a suit. The tie was loose and the top button undone, revealing some of his tattoos, but otherwise he was sleek and professional. A suit didn't seem ideal for comfort or safety on a motorcycle, but it made a pretty picture.

"Do I want to know what just made you smirk?"

I met his eyes, grinning widely. "Maybe I'll tell you later. So why'd you decide to freelance instead of working for a company?"

"Truth? I'm not good at taking orders."

"Yet you work directly with clients?"

"I know, I know. But when the boss says something, you're expected to obey, no questions asked. A client says something, and I have a chance to talk them into not being an idiot."

"True. I'm lucky my boss usually listens to us. It doesn't always do much good, but she's on our side." I shook my head. "It's the holidays, though, so no more talk about work."

I worried for a moment, as silence descended over our little table, that we wouldn't have anything else to talk about now that we'd covered the basics. But I'd forgotten how easy it had been to talk to him when we'd both been pretending to be someone else at my mother's table. Thankfully, he didn't seem to have forgotten.

"So do you like tattoos or hate them?" Logan asked.

"Huh?"

He quirked a brow. "You keep glancing at my hands and collar, and unless you've got a hand and neck thing . . ."

I paused, momentarily considering whether I did have a hand and neck thing. No, my eyes had definitely been drawn to his tattoos. One arm was covered in geometric and tribal-esque designs in black, while the other had a mix of designs that wove in and out of each other—making it hard to pin down exactly what they were, although waves seemed to have been incorporated throughout. Both tattoos didn't stop at the wrists, but swept down across the back of his hands, waves leaving a spray of black dots on one and the tribal swirls curling along the knuckles of the other.

"Isaac?"

I met his gaze. Had I been staring again? Going by his smug grin, I probably had. "Sorry, what?"

"So you like tattoos?"

"Oh, yes. And yours are exquisite."

"Got any of your own?"

It was my turn to grin. "Maybe you'll find out."

He chuckled. "That's a yes, then. I hope to—maybe—see them someday."

"Eh, it doesn't nearly stack up compared to yours." I sighed, thinking of my sparse ink. "Yours weren't youthful indulgences, were they?"

"Nope, all but one was after my rebellious stage. And trust me, if you see them, you'll be able to pick that one out."

"Embarrassing?"

"A little. Kind of a terrible design and . . ." He made a gesture that I interpreted as *overall bad*. "I'm working with my tattoo artist on something to cover it, but it has to be perfect. I want to accent it and blend it, not remove it entirely. It was still my design. That time was still part of my life, you know?" He ran a hand over his head, looking sheepish. "Though I guess you don't have tattoos you're ashamed of."

"I got mine when I was older so I didn't need parental permission. Hah, can you imagine my mom if she found out I had tattoos?"

"She doesn't know?"

"I placed it so it's not visible unless I want it to be. And I burn after a minute in the sun, so I wear one of those super-cool swimming shirts when I'm there over the summer."

"Neeerd."

"Pot, kettle."

He whistled like a teapot going off.

"She somehow hasn't seen my piercings either. Or else she's ignoring them. Or I'm that good at hiding them." I sighed, hoping we weren't about to list all of the things I was keeping from my mother.

"Sounds exhausting."

I shrugged.

"Not that you have to tell them everything. It's just . . . You love them, but are you letting them love the real you if you keep so much from them? Like, do they get to see the real you?"

I tilted my head and met his straightforward gaze. "Do you think I'm that different because you know I have ink and piercings now? I'm the same person."

Logan opened his mouth, then closed it with a grimace. "Sorry, I shouldn't be sitting here lecturing you. So, uh, see the latest Star Wars?"

Thankfully we were both nerd stereotypes enough to be able to geek out over the newest series of films—and argue how they were tweaking the universe and if it was a good or a bad thing. That led to what books we read, although he confessed he didn't do a lot of reading since he tended to fall asleep without visual stimulation. Comics were a definite, but when he did read books . . .

"Oh my god, you read romances?"

His glare across the table was firm but not yet angry. "Don't even start."

"No, no, but I never would have pegged you as a romance reader."

He shrugged his big, broad shoulders and resettled his arms on the table, making his biceps bulge, as if they were contributing to the conversation. "I like happy endings. And it covers every genre under the sun, so I can hop around and always know I'll get that happy ending—eventually. Some of them put you through the wringer. They're not all bodice rippers."

I tried not to judge. Really hard. We all had stuff we enjoyed that would get us ridiculed by others. But my brain couldn't compute the big biker dude reading *romance*.

"God, you're still thinking about it," Logan said, although laughter filled the words. "You're gonna strain yourself. Two things: one, I could be reading it for the hot sex scenes—because no genre does sex quite like romance—and also, if I'm *reading* romance, then don't you think I'll be good *involved* in romance?"

I opened my mouth, not sure what I was going to say. Unsurprisingly, nothing came out.

His smug expression returned. "See. And I know it's fiction, but I think it's nice when someone reads romance. Shows that they want that happy ending in their life."

"Yeah, after everything falls apart first."

He chuckled. "Like every other book? It'd make a boring read if nothing fell apart."

"True. Though I do have some slice-of-life manga that don't have huge amounts of conflict. Simply people going about their everyday lives and what happens. I mean, there's little conflicts, but not the drama you see on sitcoms. But I think you've won me over. Not sure I'll start reading it . . ."

I stopped, brow raised, and he smirked. "I won't force you, but I bet I could give some recommendations that would change your mind."

I thought about how much I hated the heroes in those stories always falling for the heroines—or, I supposed, the other way around—and how much it distracted from the plot. I couldn't imagine enjoying books where there was nothing but girls falling for guys and fucking. I wrinkled my nose. "You'll have to work harder on that."

His dark eyes brightened, and he sat up a little straighter. "That sounds like an offer of a second date."

Another date hadn't crossed my mind. We were both having so much fun that obviously we'd see each other again. "I'm all for that."

CHAPTER THREE

D ates with Logan were like potato chips: I couldn't stop with just one. And since we'd both taken off the week before New Year's, we had too much time on our hands.

"Hey, have you seen that new Studio Ghibli movie?"

"No, wanna go?"

So we went.

"I never have gotten around to going to the art museum."

"Want me to show you around?"

So we went.

One date tumbled into the next, usually on the following day. In some ways, we were moving incredibly fast—seeing each other daily—but each date was like going with a new best friend. Yes, that flare of attraction was still there, at least for me, but we kept it mellow.

Until one night we were standing on the front steps of my apartment building, the wind blocked by the little alcove, our breaths forming a cloud between us.

I peered up at him, stepping closer, until I could almost feel the heat radiating from his body. "I had a really nice time tonight."

He slid a hand onto my hip, then curled it around to press against my lower back, drawing me ever nearer. "So did I."

"And we're on for tomorrow?" I tilted my head up, offering my lips to him as I tried not to tremble with excitement.

"Yes. Though I'm not done thinking about tonight." He met my lips with his. They were warm, slightly rough from the cold, and the kiss was nearly chaste, a question, asking permission, opening a conversation.

I answered by parting my lips and welcoming him in. His tongue caressed the seam of my lips, teasing, not yet giving me a taste. I slid my hand up his chest, over the folds of wool and fluffy scarf, until I hooked my hand around the back of his neck.

He smiled against my lips, and my own tongue darted out to catch a hint of it. It was just as delightful as I'd expected—a tingling spark like Pop Rocks. With the added benefit that my tongue lured his back, until he was taking a taste of me and giving a taste of himself.

Heat poured through me like mulled wine, running down my spine, flooding through my limbs. I didn't feel the cold anymore, just his firm body molded to me, the warmth of our embrace, the hand pressed to my back, and the one trailing along my jaw. I felt nothing but him.

The kisses lingered, starting like embers and flaring to life, burning hotter as each one led into the next, until I shoved him against the hard brick wall. The kiss deepened as I pushed my tongue into his mouth, drinking down his flavor and reveling in it. I could get drunk off this.

The hand on my back tightened, drawing my hips to his and fanning the flames between us. I gripped his neck, pulling back from the kiss only to gasp in heavy breaths. His dark eyes glittered in the streetlights, and he looked as stunned as I felt. No, not stunned. Astounded. I slipped my thumb along his neck, tracing the softest parts where his pulse hammered. He shivered and brushed his lips against mine.

"Is this a kiss good night?" I murmured.

"I think it'd better be."

I huffed a laugh against his mouth. "Gonna leave me wanting?"

"Leave us both looking forward to tomorrow." Gently, after another kiss, he backed me off him and pulled his arms away. I expected the cold to immediately wrap around me and sneak into all the pockets of heat he'd made, but the fire still burned in my chest.

"Until tomorrow, then," I said with the sappiest smile. Then I reached up and stole one more kiss.

The next night we went to a local band's show, which was mostly an excuse to listen to music, dance ridiculously close together, and pretty much dry-hump each other in public—not that I was much aware of anyone around us.

And then it was New Year's Eve's eve. That's December thirtieth, in case you were confused. The night was dark and crisp, tasting of snow despite the forecast only calling for flurries. It was wintery and magical. As we stepped inside the restaurant, the heat blasting against my chilled cheeks, everything felt like it was going to be perfect.

I approached the podium, where a waifish young man stood, suit impeccable. "Reservation for Landes for two."

His brow scrunched and his eyes dropped, skimming through the list he had, then skimming through again, slower. He bit his lip and met my gaze. "Um, I'm sorry, sir, but I'm not finding your name. Are you sure you made a reservation?"

I was absolutely certain I'd made a reservation. Logan and I had been discussing restaurants and our favorite dishes, and I'd gushed over Être Nourri's roast duck with ginger and he'd said we should go here next. So I'd called, reserving the day before New Year's, figuring it would be less crazy. Judging by the noise and the well-dressed crowd in the entryway, the date hadn't worked in my favor. "Yes, I'm sure I made a reservation for tonight. Can you please check again?"

Anger was swelling in my chest, but I tried to keep it out of my voice. It wasn't this kid's fault that my reservation had gotten lost—Well, it probably wasn't.

Logan wrapped his hand around my elbow and tugged gently. "Hey, it's no big deal, we can come some other time."

"I made a reservation," I snapped, then immediately winced. I was getting far too pissed about missing that duck.

"I believe you." He grinned, very devil-may-care, and patted the air with his hands. With his fitted suit emphasizing his broad shoulders and letting a few tattoos peek out, I was getting less interested in the duck by the minute.

"Sorry." I huffed. "I'm getting hangry."

"Um, sir," the maître d' squeaked.

I tried not to glare at him and managed to not sound murderous when I said, "Yes?"

"Um, I see a reservation for Landes for two, next week at this time."

"I didn't make—" I clicked my teeth shut and inhaled noisily through my nose. Logan squeezed my arm, and I exhaled slowly.

"Well, I made my reservation for tonight, but there must have been a mistake when it was taken down. It happens. I'll take the reservation next week. Thank you for being so thorough. We'll be going."

Behind his cheerful smile, the guy looked like he'd avoided a beheading. "Thank you for your patience, sir. I'm extremely sorry about the confusion. I'll make sure that you have complimentary desserts then."

"Thank you." I turned and walked out, Logan right by my side.

The cool night air felt bitter against my cheeks as we headed down the street toward his car. We'd barely gone half a block when I pulled up short, tilted my head back, and shouted, "Goddamn motherfucker!"

The pressure on my chest lifted; the boiling anger washed away. And then Logan was standing there, towering over me. He met my gaze, passion flaring in his expression. It made his eyes shimmer and my skin warm. He slid his hands into my hair, lowered his face, and kissed me. Despite the firm grip he had on my hair, his lips were soft and open, deepening the kiss without demanding. The last remnants of my icy frustration melted under his touch. After a few kisses, he wrapped his arms around me, and then he murmured, as if we hadn't just been kissing, "Are you done scaring all the other pedestrians?"

"Yes. Sorry. I've no idea why that set me off like that." My stomach grumbled, as if it knew exactly why.

"Hey, you didn't scream at the host, and I think the night sky can take it. Let's go grab some Chinese food and head back to my place. We can even order duck." He grinned.

"Asshole." Though I was excited to see his apartment.

The grin broke into a chuckle. "They might have some very good duck!" He kissed my nose. "And now we know what our plans are for next week."

"Oh shit, I said we'd be there! You probably have plans with your friends—"

"No, I'm totally free. Unless you don't want to have dinner with me." He blinked his big eyes at me like some moe anime girl. It looked better on him.

"Of course I want to have dinner with you. I was hoping to have it tonight." I wrinkled my nose.

He kissed it again. "Good. Then let's get going."

We ordered the Chinese food on the phone as we walked to his place, and arrived when the delivery guy did. As if the world was trying to make up for one obstacle by having the solution go so smoothly.

Inside we shucked our jackets and coats, rolled up our sleeves—I had a feeling he'd done it to tease me with his ink, while I was trying to keep the sauces off the whites—and sat down to dinner at the kitchen table.

His apartment was pretty much what I expected: the basic white walls covered by framed art, most of it illustrated like comic books, but a few classics in the vein of Escher and Hokusai. Everything was neater than I'd thought it would be—not that I'd thought he'd be a slob, but most bachelors I knew tended not to tidy as often as they should. He had a vibrant red blanket folded over the back of his plush, dark-brown couch, and the accompanying pillows were tucked into the corners where they belonged. Nothing was dusty, and the carpet was fairly clean. But his coffee table was covered in clutter, and dirty dishes were stacked by the sink, so he probably wasn't a neat-freak.

He opened up the container with the duck-something-or-other that he'd ordered. "Want the duck?"

"I hate you." I held out my plate so it was closer to the container. "Yes."

Grinning, he scooped some onto my plate.

No, the duck at China Inn wasn't as good as the duck at Être Nourri, but it wasn't a disappointment either. That might have been because I barely paid attention to what I was eating while we talked and joked. It didn't matter that we were all dressed up with nowhere to go. We'd found a place to go. Even if it ended up being a small apartment downtown with delivery takeout.

After eating too much and putting away the leftovers, we made our way to his living room and couch with plans to watch a movie. Instead, he pulled me from the stacks of DVDs to the couch, as I put up a half-hearted fight, then tugged me onto his lap. I wasn't a waifish maître d', but his legs could handle me, and the firm muscles provided a cushion as I landed and fell against his chest.

I laughed, slinging my arm over the back of the couch and tucking it behind his head, drawing our faces closer. Better to take advantage of the position, right? "What? Am I some damsel in distress now?"

His hands slid around my waist, one ending up low on my hip, the other spreading high across my thigh, the thumb dangerously— deliciously?—close to my crotch. "I think the only thing you'd need saved from is yourself. I rather like that about you."

"Mmm. I think I should be offended." I squirmed a little closer and pressed my lips to his. They were still salty and sweet from dinner, but it was no hardship to search deeper to get a taste of him. The hand on my hip squeezed, holding me securely as his tongue caressed mine. I hummed against his mouth, and then my smile broke our kiss as his left hand nudged higher. "And where is that hand headed, Mr. Mazza?"

He pressed his thumb against the bulge at my zipper, not quite stroking. "Just getting a lay of the land."

"A *lay* of the land?" I snickered, and he groaned.

"Puns are the death of erections, you know."

"Mm-hmm?" I grazed my free hand down his chest to where his groin was wedged by my thigh. The angle was awkward, but I could rub the heel of my hand against his cock.

He inhaled sharply, and I shifted to give my hand room to work, melting that hiss into a moan.

"My touch must have revitalizing powers, then."

He gave a breathy chuckle as his own fingers grew more insistent on my dick, matching my tease stroke for stroke. "Yeah, a regular Phoenix Down."

It was my turn to groan against his lips. "Oh god, Final Fantasy sex talk. I'm not sure if that's going to get you kicked out or laid."

His palm folded heat over the growing bulge in my pants and rubbed with the perfect amount of pressure. "We both know this is my place."

"I guess that only leaves one option, then."

"I guess it does."

In a feat of agility that I'd never had before—at least not without someone getting smacked in the face accidentally—I twisted us sideways so he was stretched along the sofa and I was straddling him.

The hand that had been around his neck was now propping me up while I caressed the other up his chest to tease his nipple.

His cheeks were flushed and his eyes wide, like he hadn't expected this turn of events—pun intended. I leaned down, grinning wickedly. "Now you're all laid."

"Oh god, that's terrible—"

I thrust my hips, and he gasped. I licked my lips. "Terrible?"

"Okay, maybe not so bad." His hands found their new position on my ass, guiding me to rock my hips, squeezing, digging in a little through my slacks.

"Mmm, I thought so." I followed the rhythm he set, keeping it slow and sensual as I lowered my lips to his. This wasn't much different from what we'd done on the dance floor—although this time we were horizontal and there seemed to be a promise of an orgasm at the end.

One that didn't involve me alone in bed thinking of him.

My fingers brushed over his nipple again, this time finding the peaked nub through his shirt and pinching.

He grunted, his hands tightening, breaking our rhythm and the kiss. "Not that."

"No?"

He shook his head without moving more than an inch. "Rub, lick, lips, but no biting or pinching. It's, like, actually reverse arousing."

"Noted." A kiss. "Definitely don't want to do that." Instead I traced my fingers to the buttons of his shirt and began undoing them. After all, it was hard to lick a nipple through a shirt. He had an undershirt on, but with some cooperation, I was able to push it up out of the way.

Immediately I was distracted from his nipples by the ink that sprawled from his shoulders down the sides of his torso, accenting his obliques with matched waves of tribal-esque swirls. "Oh fuck."

He moaned, possibly because I'd stopped moving, and his fingers began to fiddle with my fly. "Something wrong?"

"I forgot that I get to explore all of this." I pulled out of his grip—which was a shame, because he'd almost had his hand in my briefs—and slid down his body until my mouth was positioned at the bottom point of the tattoo, right above the waist of his pants. "Not ticklish, are you?"

He chuckled breathlessly. "Think I would have been able to get this tattoo if I was?"

"Good." I traced the thick lines of ink with my lips and tongue, following the curves over muscles that rippled beneath the teasing touch and tensed when I stopped to suck—or nip—a particularly tasty bit.

"Fuck," he whispered, one hand grabbing my shoulder, the other fisting itself in my hair. He didn't direct me where to go, only held on, like he needed to be grounded as my mouth traveled.

"You can pull if you'd like," I murmured against his pec before my lips abandoned the tattoo to play over his nipple.

"Fuck," was his response, and his fingers tightened, once again tugging without commanding.

The slight ache slithered down my spine and nestled in my groin. *Fuck* was right. His grip was perfect. I hummed my approval against his skin, wetting his nipple with a kiss and then blowing cool air on it to watch it tighten. His sensitivity was something I'd need to explore more, but at the moment, there was an urgent matter at hand: the constraint of our pants.

With his shirts covering the rest of the tattoos, I dropped down, passing all that lovely muscled torso until my lips sealed over his belly button while my fingers undid his zipper. Pushing through the opening, his cock strained against his briefs. I glanced down and amusement curled my lips.

"Do you seriously have a Mario mushroom on your underwear?"

"Shit." He groaned. "I forgot I was wearing those."

I muffled my snicker against his groin, pressing into the hard-on.

"Jesus," he whispered, his voice hitching. "Uh, yeah, the back says 'Eat me and I'll make you grow.'"

My snickers got worse.

He massaged my scalp with his fingers. "Seemed like a good idea at the time?"

"Well, better test the theory."

"What do you—"

But I'd already tugged his underwear down, releasing his cock to wrap my lips around it.

"Fuck!"

I slid my mouth down, taking him as deep as I could. His cockhead bumped against the back of my throat, the width enough that I knew I'd ache by the end of this. I was looking forward to it.

And, by the way, his underwear was accurate: eating him did make me grow.

I pulled back until only his head was in my mouth, lips tight around the neck, choking it while my tongue played over the slit. I dropped my hands to my own pants, hastily pushing down my far-less-amusing underwear to free my cock. The first touch of air was refreshingly cool, which made my hand feel like a hot brand when I fisted my cock. I muffled my moan by filling my throat with his dick.

"Yes," he groaned. "Hell. You're touching yourself, aren't you? Fuck, that's hot." He groaned again as I accidentally let my teeth brush a little too close against his skin on an upstroke. "Damn it, Isaac."

I wasn't sure why he was damning me, unless he liked ending the night with blue balls. I sucked harder instead of asking.

"Yes," he whispered, and then his head smacked against the sofa cushion. "Fuck. No."

His words were conflicting, but his hands released me to grab under my arms and drag me up before I could back off on my own. His cock slipped from my mouth with a wet *pop*, and I had to let go of my own to catch myself as my lips fell against his.

In between kisses, he panted, "If you keep that up, I'll come." I rather thought that was the point, but he purred, "And as much as I'd love to fuck your mouth, tonight I want you up here. With me."

Before I could say a thing, his large hand wrapped around both of our cocks, pressing them together in that tight heat, slicked by my spit. The other hand grabbed my ass and started me rocking, not that I needed much encouragement. The new position wasn't as intense as my hand on my cock, his in my mouth, but the slide of his hand, the bumps and ridges as our cocks rubbed together, was intimate. A slow, steady fuck rather than a rush to orgasm, his one hand setting the pace, the other squeezing a little with every perfect thrust.

The shivers of anticipation started as a tightness in my balls, then spread with a sharp explosion when I came, thrusting hard against him, prolonging my orgasm. He cried out as I kept shuddering, and

I let my body be guided by his hands, falling to the side when he indicated the contact was too much.

I panted against his chest, my face tucked between his shoulder and neck. There was some movement, and then he rubbed along my back with a clean hand.

"You okay?"

I laughed as another shiver rocked through me, my exhausted muscles quivering. "Um, yeah."

"That was kinda great."

"'Kinda'?" I snorted. "How about 'pretty damn'?"

He kissed my temple, his breath warm as he said, "You're right. That was pretty damn great."

"Mmm," I agreed, then shifted so I was less straddling him and more lying along him, our bodies folded together on the small space of the sofa, wrapped in the heat of sex. There would be a chill later as the exertion wore off, but for now I could stay here forever.

It was an amazing and terrifying thought.

CHAPTER FOUR

"I'm sorry we're all abandoning you for New Year's," Jackson, one of my best friends, said over the phone. He currently sounded like Darth Vader—including the interspersed heavy breathing.

"It's okay—"

"You're only saying that because my kid didn't get you sick!"

"Well, yeah. But what did you expect when you had your toddler around everyone for Christmas? They're little breeding grounds for sick. But as much as I wish I was ringing in the new year with you guys, I, uh, sorta met someone."

"Oh? In the five days I've been dead to the world?"

"Pretty much." I could feel the heat in my cheeks, although I knew Jackson and Emmett had gone from meeting to married in a very short time. "I met him right after Christmas, and since all of my friends had to cancel their plans with me this week, I spent all my time with him. It was fun. And he invited me to go hang with his people on New Year's Eve."

"Oh, meeting the friends already?"

"Jeez. First you abandon me, then you heckle me for making other plans."

Jackson gave a throaty laugh that sounded more like death than amusement. "Sorry. Go have fun. I'm just excited our little Zack is all grown up."

Sigh. "You're an asshole, you know that?"

"Okay, okay, I'll stop." Another phlegmy chuckle. "I am excited you met someone though. I hope New Year's Eve goes well."

"Thanks. I hope you and Emmett and Rosa feel better."

"Sure. We'll ring in the new year by being unconscious in bed. Parenting is fun."

"Look at your life; look at your choices."

"I do. Every day. No regrets."

"You're disgustingly happy." I stuck my tongue out at the phone.

"Hey, I want all my friends disgustingly happy too."

"And sick, it seems," I couldn't help adding.

"If love is a sickness, then I don't want to be well!"

I snorted. "Okay, I think your cold meds have kicked in. Say good night, Gracie."

"Good night, Shirley."

I had no clue what he was talking about. The drugs must have hit him hard. I lowered the phone and texted in the group chat that I hoped everyone had a good new year and felt better, and that despite them abandoning me, I had plans. They didn't rib me much—they probably figured Jackson would have already—and asked for all the details.

I told them the bare facts, trying not to gush. I wasn't superstitious or anything, but it felt risky to say how awesome Logan was when we hadn't known each other that long. It was hard not to, though, because he was awesome, and after last night, everything felt *right*.

Jenna demanded: *We better get pics.*

<3 If only so we know who to hunt down, Laura, her girlfriend, said.

Definitely not to judge your taste in men, Mark said.

Roe admitted, *I will totally be judging.*

You will not be disappointed, I promised. It had only been a week, so I didn't have any couple-selfies. I didn't think that would give the best angle anyway, although it would show his broadness. Would he find it odd if I insisted on taking a picture of him? Preferably shirtless.

The thought was still on my mind as Logan picked me up in his car and we headed to his friends' place. Not that envisioning Logan shirtless was a hardship. But a picture? It depended on how the evening went—the involvement of booze could go a long way toward getting a man's shirt off, as I knew from personal experience. Not that I had plans to get him drunk and take advantage of him. Well, maybe for the topless pictures, which, when phrased that way, did sound pretty skeevy.

Sigh. Okay, no sneaky shirtless pics were happening. I'd have to see if he'd pose for me anyway. Shirt optional.

"You're smirking again," Logan said as we walked down the street toward his friend's place. "I thought you'd be nervous about meeting everyone, but there you are grinning like a maniac."

I snorted. "I *had* managed to distract myself. *Now* I'm nervous. Thanks."

"Nothing to be nervous about." He used his hold on my hand to tug me closer so our shoulders bumped.

"Then why did you think I would be?"

"Uh . . ." He chuckled, then affected Ackbar's voice. "It's a trap."

I shivered. That voice shouldn't be sexy, but it also didn't seem possible for Logan to make a voice that wasn't sexy. This was a twisty, confusing experience. "Well, I had been thinking about what I'd need to do to get you shirtless so I could take pictures to send to my friends to make them all jealous, but . . ."

"I volunteer as tribute."

I pulled him down to kiss his cheek, honestly amazed that we didn't bash heads. "You're a brave man."

Truth be told, I was extremely nervous about meeting his friends. Because these weren't just his friends. They were his *family*. Sure, he'd met my family, but that had been on a lark; he hadn't been trying to impress them. Had been trying the opposite, actually. I, however, was going into the lion's den with the people who were most important to Logan.

No pressure.

"See, this is what I expected as we headed to the party," he said, knocking on the front door of a townhouse. "Terrified silence."

I took a deep breath and held it a second. "Thanks."

"Don't worry, it'll be fine. I'm the pickiest one in the group, I swear. And you passed my muster, so you must be okay."

"Oh good, I'm 'okay.'"

He was still snickering when the door opened and a dark-skinned, curly-haired woman was standing there. Immediately her mouth split open in a huge smile. "Logan!"

Her gaze shifted to me and raked over my body like I was naked and she could see every blemish. Although, based on the gleam in her eye, maybe she wasn't looking at blemishes. "And your guest."

"I'll introduce him to everyone once you let us inside." He nudged the door with the toe of his shoe.

She stepped aside, holding the door wide and making a sweeping gesture with her arm. "*Entrez vous, s'il vous plaît.*"

"Oooh, a fancy French restaurant." I clamped my hands around Logan's arm like ladies always did when they were excited in rom-coms. And it wasn't only to hide the slight nervous tremor in my hands. "Logan, why didn't you tell me? I would have dressed better!"

Logan rolled his eyes as we stepped in, but the young woman who'd opened the door was giggling as she closed it behind us. "I hate to disappoint, mysterious stranger, but that's all the French I know. Though there will be, uh, apéritifs and hors d'oeuvres."

I let go of Logan's arm to clap, hamming it up and earning a grin from her. Then I slipped out of my jacket, and Logan took the coat, eyes rolling again. Still? He handed the jackets to our host, who hung them in a closet full of tangled shoes.

"Okay," she said, "let's go introduce your cutie to everyone else."

I slipped my hand into Logan's, not wanting to be clingy but needing something to settle the nerves that were rocketing through my body. He squeezed my hand and threw me a smile as we climbed a short set of steps and turned into a living room packed with people. Okay, not wall-to-wall packed, but the seats were all filled and a few people were standing by a table that was weighed down with food. I was glad we'd decided to bring champagne.

"Okay, everyone!" our host announced. "Logan is here with his arm candy. Time for introductions." She turned to me. "There will be a test later, of course."

"Of course," I said. Although I hoped everyone wasn't expecting much from me. My name-face recall was awful. Like, if I hadn't been eye-fucking Logan on our first meeting, I would have forgotten his name in the first half an hour. It was bad.

"My name's Erika," our host said, and then she pointed around the room, throwing out names at such speed that I barely had time to repeat them once in my head before she was moving on to the next person. She was grinning when she finished. "Now it's your turn."

"Okay." I pointed at myself. "My name's Erika."

It got the laughs I was going for, even from Logan. He dragged me farther into the room and made more personal introductions. The crowd was friendly, although it felt like as soon as anyone said one word to Logan, they slipped into a foreign language—and it wasn't French. There were references to shows I hadn't seen, experiences I hadn't been present for, topics I knew nothing about. Nothing strange when meeting new people. I clung to Logan so I wouldn't float away on a sea of unfamiliarity. It was probably normal new-person jitters.

Thankfully as we went around, he made a point to say which were his "best friends" versus just "friends," giving me a clue they were important and I should remember them. I only hoped I could: Erika, Jacob, Bryan, Troy, Alessa, and Matti. I tried to lock them in. It was a blessing his friends were varied and colorful, so at least they weren't twelve blonde sorority sisters I'd need to tell apart.

Eventually we ended up on a couch, plates of food balanced on our knees, drinks cluttering the coffee table.

"All I'm saying is, it's been a hell of a year," Erika said. "I know nothing changes at the strike of midnight, but I want to wash away all of it."

"All of it?" Alessa asked from her spot on the floor by Erika's feet, head angled up, a teasing smile on her lips.

"Well. I guess getting together with you was a good thing."

"Wow. Thanks." Alessa turned her head and bit Erika's knee.

"Hey!" Erica gently smacked the back of Alessa's head. "I said it was a good thing!"

"You *guess.*" Alessa pouted and Erika bent down. I averted my gaze as they shared a disgustingly sweet kiss.

I focused on Logan instead, who was smirking and watching me. He leaned over to murmur in my ear, "What do you think so far?"

I bussed my lips against his cheek and whispered back, "They are terrifying and wonderful."

His hum rippled down my spine and settled in my groin, not at all helped by his warm hand landing on my thigh, above the plate, and giving a squeeze. "I'm glad you approve."

"Aww, the cute new couple is being all couple-y."

Logan glared at Troy—well, I thought it was Troy. "Fuck off. You're just jealous."

Troy grabbed his chest in mock hurt. "I would deny it, were it not true."

The banter slipped into talks about the shitty past year—filled with inside jokes that flew over my head and cutting comments that made me wince—hopes for the new one, and plans for resolutions, most of which seemed to be variations of "last year's resolutions, but actually do them."

Erika turned to me, eyes sparkling. "So, Isaac, what's your resolution?"

"The usual: lose weight, make millions, have a hot biker fall madly in love with me." The hand on my thigh squeezed again, and I couldn't help smiling. "I have high hopes."

"Good luck with that last one," Alessa chimed, and everyone started talking at once—I couldn't quite follow what was being said, mostly because the hand on my thigh had inched up a little bit more.

"I have high hopes too" was whispered in my ear with such promise that I felt like a fool: one week and I was falling hard.

But at least he seemed to be falling with me.

"Four!"
"Three!"
"Two!"
"One!"

"Happy mummmum . . ." My greeting to the new year was muffled as Logan covered my mouth with his lips. Damn could he kiss. Not only with his lips and tongue, but his hands, his breath, his entire body molding against me and drawing me into it until I gladly submitted to whatever he wanted. And what he wanted to do was kiss. If we weren't at his friend's house, we probably would have dropped to the couch and gone further—our hands were already creeping toward skin—but we didn't. Even though I wanted to wrap my legs around him and go at it.

He broke the kiss, whispering, "Happy New Year," against my lips while I panted and tried not to hump his leg, which I'd straddled at some point.

"Happy New Year," I managed between breaths, staring up into his dark eyes. "A very nice start to the year."

"I think it promises to be a good one."

He pressed his lips to mine again, stealing my breath away once more, and I knew he was right.

CHAPTER FIVE

I woke slowly, wrapped in warmth. Logan was beside me, still smelling faintly of cologne. I'd gone home with him the night before, plans of fucking like bunnies forefront in my mind as we got into the car. But as we drove the relatively short distance to his place, the hum of the champagne, the purr of the car, and the lateness of the hour had worked together to drag my eyelids farther and farther down. By the time we brushed our teeth and stripped out of our clothes, my kisses had been sleepy. The heat of our bodies cocooned in the blanket had been the final nudge that pushed me into sleep.

But now I felt rejuvenated. And other things. As much as I didn't want to, I slipped from the bed and made a quick escape to the bathroom. I did my business and was back under the covers before Logan woke up, my spot still warm if not my hands. I gave them a moment before I succumbed to the urge to touch him. Up his arms, tracing tattoos hidden from view by blankets; across his shoulders, following the swoop of his muscles; teasing down his pecs, the ridges of his abdomen, to rest above the abundance of dark curls.

"Mmm" vibrated through him, rumbling beneath my fingers and shooting like a charge through me. "I see you're awake now."

I kissed his shoulder and used my leverage to press our bodies together, one leg creeping over him, my groin telling him that I was very much up. "Yes, I'm sorry I fell asleep last night."

A chuckle. No one should be able to sound that filthy first thing in the morning. "I wore you out."

I snorted. "That you did. But luckily I seem to have recovered."

"You have." He rolled onto his back, sliding an arm around me and playing his fingers up my spine, over the circuit-board tattoo he loved so much. His eyes were crinkled with sleep, and wrinkles were imprinted into his cheek from the sheets. I couldn't help brushing my fingers along those grooves, and he smiled. "What ever shall we do with our day?"

"Well, it's a New Year's tradition in my family to have pork and sauerkraut."

"With mashed potatoes?"

"Always."

"Mmm, sounds good." He rocked us over, his weight pressing me into the mattress, his lips against mine, recalling the first kiss we'd shared in the new year. Heat sparked through me, and all thoughts of dinner—or breakfast and lunch, for that matter—fled.

I spread my legs to cradle his body, and hugged him with my thighs as each kiss bled into another, lips and tongues dancing together. I gripped his shoulders, the hot skin on one side of my hands, the cool air on the other. Sliding one hand to the back of his neck, I kept him there—not that he was trying to move away—and took control of the kiss. As much as I wanted the explosive passion his lips promised, I had some exploring I wanted to do first.

When I managed to break the kiss, I used my weight—and his cooperation—to roll us over so I was on top, my hands pinning his shoulders and our hips locked together in the most perfect way. Well, maybe the second most perfect way. Or third. I could think of a few other positions . . .

I was getting distracted. It wasn't hard to get distracted by him, an expanse of tan, tattooed skin rippling with muscle beneath me.

"See," I said, apropos of nothing, "if we'd met in the summer, I wouldn't have to put off the rigorous fucking."

He smirked. "'Rigorous fucking'? You have a way with language."

I rubbed my cock against his, using his groin to cut off his words with a gasp. "I have a need to see all your tattoos. Up close."

In case he wasn't sure how close I meant, I raised his right arm to my lips and kissed his knuckles.

"Have at me."

I started on the arm with the intricate designs because I wasn't stupid. There was a good chance I'd get involved in what I was doing and begin to rush. And if I missed anything, I wanted it to be the tribal designs and not the ones that needed studied. Not that I'd actually get through them all this morning.

I brushed my lips over the smattering of sea spray, then slid to his wrist and nibbled at the bone. When I'd had my fill, I turned it over to follow the swell of waves to a mark on the inside. It was a shooting star, the trail melting into the waves. I was tempted to ask what it meant. If it held meaning. But there would be time for that. We'd known each other a week, and he had a lot of tattoos. I couldn't expect the story behind each one right now.

The fingers of his other hand curled into my hair. "What are you thinking?"

"That I look forward to learning all your stories." I kissed the shooting star and followed the current to the next one: a dragon wrapped around his forearm, the head nestled on his elbow.

"They don't all have deep, meaningful histories, you know."

"I figured." I kissed the head of the dragon. "But I bet most of them do."

"Well, all the *good* ones do."

I hit upon a strange duck, its beak open to reveal razor-sharp teeth. It wasn't *bad*, but the art wasn't nearly as good as everything else I'd come across so far. "And this one?"

"Yeah, that's the one I'm thinking of fixing up. It's to tell the world to duck off."

"Oh my god."

"Uh-huh. I wish I could say there was booze involved, but my tattoo artist would never do that. I was stone-cold sober at the time."

A giggle bubbled out of my chest and spilled across the ferocious avian. "It has a certain charm."

I shifted to move up his arm, and our bare cocks bumped and slid together, pulling sounds of pleasure from both of us. The hand in my hair tightened. "You need to study every tattoo right now?"

I thrust my hips in our new position and pleasure sizzled over my skin. I raised my head from its spot by his shoulder. "You could possibly persuade me otherwise."

"Oh? I wonder how I could do that." The fingers loosened their grip on my hair and coursed down my body, trailing goose bumps in their wake before wrapping around my cock. "What have we here?"

I moaned as his hand stroked up. "It's your New Year's present." Groaning, this time in pain, I let my forehead smack against his shoulder. "Sorry, that was terrible and I deserve to be punished."

He cackled as he released my cock and flipped us over, pinning me to the bed. "I think not being able to kiss every tattoo this morning will be a good punishment."

I squirmed, enough to free my legs to spread for him, giving him a place between them. My thighs rested on either side of his hips. Heat flared through my body, but I couldn't resist a playful grin. "Oh yes, punish me."

He muffled his snort of laughter on my neck. It tickled, yet it made me quake with desire too. But maybe that was because the chuckles became kisses, his breath warm and moist as he rocked against me. "I dunno, you seem a little too eager to be punished."

"And a discussion about kinky sex and safewords shouldn't happen naked in bed."

He froze, then rose up, far enough that I could see his dark, hungry eyes. He stared down at me, studying me a moment, then kissed me. "Right."

A shiver slunk down my spine, half lust, half fear. "If you're into that sort of thing."

He dropped his mouth to my ear, whispering kisses there. "As you said, a discussion for when we're not in bed about to fuck."

"Fucking? Is that what we're—" He cut off my snark with a well-placed thrust. I gasped and arched beneath him. "Hell."

"I'd prefer heaven, thanks." He nibbled his way along my neck.

I tilted my head, giving him all the access he wanted. And he took. God, did he take. But each inch he stole gave me another inch.

I groaned at my own bad pun.

"Don't like that?" he asked against my collarbone.

"It's wonderful. My brain is being mean and making terrible puns."

He chuckled. I'd never known someone who laughed so much in bed. Of course, I'd rarely met someone who'd put up with my jokes for this long when there were straining erections between us, either. He kissed my breastbone. "Well, if you can still think up bad puns, I must not be doing my job."

He doubled down. He went for my right nipple and didn't hesitate to hook his teeth on the bar pierced there. One tug and I arched, my breath ripped from my lungs as all the blood rushed into my cock.

"Oh fuck. Puns forgotten," I panted.

He let go and swiped his tongue over hot skin and metal, soothing the abused flesh. "Mmm, good. Let's see if the other side is as effective."

"Oh, it is—" I inhaled sharply as his teeth latched on to the matching bar. He didn't pull this time, though, simply sank his pearly whites in a little more as fire burst from the contact and spread across my skin.

The initial pain—and yes, it was pain even though it made my cock leak against my stomach—was followed by his lips sealing around the peaked flesh and sucking. I might have blacked out from the pleasure. I definitely didn't remember wrapping my legs around his hips and starting to hump him.

Sex was rarely a dignified activity, but I felt especially debauched this morning. Yet, I regretted nothing except his mouth pulling away.

"Fuck, you look . . ." He didn't say how I looked, but by the rough growl of need in his voice, I could guess.

I released the sheets, which I hadn't realized I'd been holding, and clamped down on his shoulders again. "Fucking. Yes. Please."

He rose up and shifted to the side, but didn't get very far—my legs and hands were in a vise grip around him. Our groins rubbed in glorious friction, and he sank back down, seeking out my mouth for a sloppy kiss. "You need to let me go if you want fucking to happen."

Oh, I wanted. It still took a moment for my brain to issue the orders and for my legs and arms to obey. Finally they let go and his heat left me. Only briefly though. Then he was once more a blanket of need over me, mouth claiming mine as if he'd missed the kisses as much as I had.

"Where were we?" He hummed against my lips.

"I think you were about to fuck me into the mattress." I figured he'd forgive me the cliché; it was all his fault I couldn't think.

"Yes." He dipped beneath the covers again, his mouth finding my nipple, although he strummed rather than pulled it taut, and his hands searched between my splayed legs. A dry touch, like his fingers were on a scouting expedition, learning the lay of the land, teasing me endlessly. Then they left, there was a quiet squirt, and they returned, a little chilly and very slippery.

They knew exactly where to go.

A single slender digit slipped in, not much more than a caress. He traced the rim, then delved deeper, waking up and stretching the muscles. His kisses trailed their way up to my mouth, and his tongue thrust in as a second finger did. He devoured my moans as his fingers worked slowly and surely. Driving me mad.

He added a third, and I begged, "Please."

"'Please'?" he echoed, the word barely an exhale. His fingers twisted, either by design or goddamn luck, and pleasure shot through me.

"Fuck!" Everything in me tightened around him, trying to hold him there to keep that pleasure coming. "Right there. Please. Fuck me."

His laugh was breathless. "I can't stay right here *and* fuck you."

I growled and bit his lip. Harder than I'd intended, but he didn't seem to mind. "If you don't fuck me this instant, I'm going to come on your fingers and leave you with blue balls."

He froze, his fingers barely not touching my prostate, his dark eyes wide and his interest visible. "That's . . . that's hotter than it should be."

"Fine." I growled again and thrust against his fingers, sending another wave of pleasure through me.

"Oh no you don't." He pulled his fingers out and leaned back, taking a moment to roll on the condom and spread some lube on it. I waited impatiently. Then he positioned himself and pressed the head of his cock against my hole.

I relaxed and bore down. The head entered, stretching me in a way his fingers couldn't. The widest part breached the ring of muscles and the pleasure doubled, the initial ache settling into heat. He pushed in with a slow, rocking progress as my body accepted his width. Resting his weight on his hands, he lowered his forehead to mine, our eyes locked. And then he was all the way in, his hips flush to my ass, our bodies joined. My breath caught as I stared up at him. His eyes were wide and his cheeks were flushed.

Fuck, he was gorgeous.

I tilted my chin up, silently asking, and he answered with the desired kiss. It was almost delicate and sweet despite the earlier dirty talk. It was fresh air, and I could breathe again.

"Fuck me."

He pulled out and then thrust in hard and fast. My back arched and my eyes closed. Not because I didn't want to see the hunger in his gaze, but because I simply couldn't keep them open. A whispered yes hissed from between my lips, and he did it again. He set a rhythm that gave me no hope of holding back a litany of curses and gasps, and far too soon my climax was approaching.

"Yes, fuck, yes!"

He must have heard something in those words, the bastard, because he thrust in, balls to my ass, and stopped.

I opened my eyes. He loomed above me, sweat glistening on his skin, his pupils as blown as I imagined mine were, his nostrils flaring with every heavy breath. But all of that faded with the need teetering in my balls. Another thrust and I'd come in an explosion between us.

Still, he stared down at me.

"Move," I begged, my voice little more than a whine.

He licked his lips, his gaze tracking to my mouth and then up again. For a moment, I didn't think he was going to reply. Maybe he hadn't heard me over our breathing. He leaned down—the slight shift inside me sending electricity over my nerves—and kissed me. Warm and soft. His words were barely a whisper. "I wish this could never end."

Sweet words. I shuddered in pleasure, clamping down on where our bodies joined. "It doesn't end. It's just waves on the shore. Sometimes it's high tide." I had no idea what I was saying, but I needed him to move and begging hadn't worked. "Please give me high tide."

"Jesus." He kissed me again, this time deep and dirty, his tongue exploring every inch that it could. He yanked his hips back and slammed forward, setting a brutal pace that lit every nerve in ecstasy.

My climax washed over me like those waves I'd spoken about, not drowning me but leaving me gasping for air as I shook with the force of it. I was always sensitive when I came without a hand on my cock, and as he continued thrusting with a new urgency, I nearly hummed with *too much*.

Right when I was about to vibrate apart with the discomfort, he pulled out. He rocked his weight onto one arm, and his face twisted in torturous need as he jerked himself off. His orgasm plastered ridiculous expressions across his face. But it didn't make me want to laugh. It made me pull him close and kiss him—his chin, his lips, his cheeks—as he gasped and twitched. With a final shudder, he collapsed in a sated pile, mostly to the side, but with one leg slung over me.

We lay there, wordless and sweaty and breathing heavily.

"Wow." All the teasing words from earlier had been fucked out of me.

His leg tightened around me, drawing me closer. His arm joined in securing me against his chest. I didn't resist. I lay there, my legs pudding. Eventually I turned my head and saw the same goofy smile on his lips as I felt on mine.

"Wow," I repeated.

"Wow," he agreed.

We stayed there, cuddling under the blankets, until our strength returned. I mostly wanted to fall back to sleep, like any good fuck made me want to do, but it was morning and we had to get out of bed at some point. Eating was a thing, after all.

That didn't mean we couldn't have a leisurely breakfast followed by a not-so-quick shower together, though. There was nothing quite like the feeling of water pouring over me as I was on my knees, giving a blowjob for all my worth before the warm water ran out.

I couldn't remember ever having a better start to the new year.

CHAPTER SIX

ating Logan was amazing. Really, what wasn't there to like? He was hot as fuck, sweet as candy, and funny as hell. After a month and a half, the initial heart-fluttering infatuation was starting to wear off, but I also got to see the real him more and more. Cute things, like the snuffling snore noises he sometimes made right before he woke up. And not-so-cute things, like when work ate up all his time.

"So what are your plans for V-day?" Jackson asked, shaking a toy in front of Rosa's face. They were playing on the floor, so I slumped down to join them.

"Don't know yet. Why, trying to wrangle me into babysitting so you can have a night out?"

"What?" Jackson smacked a pale palm to his chest like some Southern belle. "I would never. I'm only asking."

"Because Roe already agreed to babysit," Emmett added, emerging from the downstairs. "They broke up with whats-her-name, and no, they don't want to talk about it, thanks for asking. So they offered. I think they need something to distract them on the big day."

"Oooh, and what do you two have planned— No, honey, don't chew on my pants, please." I carefully removed my jeans from Rosa's mouth and hoisted her up into the air. She let out a joyous squeal.

"Honestly?" Jackson said. "We want to go out and see that movie everyone's been talking about. And we have reservations at Mama Lucy's. And then we might go shopping."

"Ah, married life is bliss."

"Fuck off." Emmett laughed.

"Language," Jackson reminded him.

Emmett winced. He'd always had a bit of a mouth on him, and it was taking time to tame it, while the baby—well, toddler—was getting closer to first-word territory. "Uh, bite me? There. Yeah, bite me."

I bopped Rosa's nose. "I'm sure she's got some chompers to assist."

"And thankfully not much jaw strength to back them up. So spill, what are you and Logan doing since you're young and in love?"

Heat flushed my cheeks at the mention of being *in love*. Not because we weren't, but because those words hadn't been said yet. I was pretty sure I loved him. Pretty sure he loved me. But I had no idea if it was too soon. And the holiday of pink and red was *not* the time to say it.

"Zack is thinking dirty thoughts!"

"I am not!" I groused, setting Rosa down facing away from me. Aiming her at Emmett and his pants as he joined us on the floor. "We haven't talked about it yet. He's been killing himself getting a bunch of projects done for this client and we're lucky if we can text, let alone see each other."

"Oh, boo. When does the project wrap?"

"Last week. Except they weren't happy with something so it got extended. But he'd already had a full plate of other projects scheduled, so now he's even more stressed. If they weren't paying him so well, I think he'd rage quit."

"Goddamn clients." Jackson winced. "I mean. Poopy-heads." He shrugged helplessly. "Well, you should plan something nice for him. Like, if he doesn't have time to go out, maybe take a fancy dinner to his place."

"With a blowjob," Emmett added.

Jackson nodded. "Blowjobs are always appreciated."

"Yeah? Would Roe agree with that?"

"Okay, let's say I'm confident Logan would appreciate a blowjob. Although we haven't met him yet, so it's hard to say." Insert meaningful look here.

"Did you hear me saying how he's been crazy busy with his project?"

"For a month?"

"Well, we were kinda new and then the project hit."

"You've met his friends," Jackson grumbled.

"Okay, okay! I swear, first weekend he's free from this project, we'll make introductions all around."

Jackson nodded approvingly and leaned forward to wipe drool from Rosa's face. "Good. 'Cause you know a relationship doesn't count until you introduce him to the family."

I tensed.

Emmett rolled his eyes. "*This* family, Zack. Not your blood family. We're way more important anyway."

I couldn't help noticing that Jackson had trained his focus on Rosa, practically pulling himself from the conversation. I dragged my gaze to Emmett. "You're better, if nothing else."

That seemed to satisfy them.

Over the next few days, I worked, talked to Logan on the phone in the evenings when he finally finished work, and plotted Valentine's Day. I didn't expect that it would be perfect, but it would be as perfect as circumstances would allow, and that seemed most important.

On the day of, I texted him at three to let him know I'd be bringing dinner over, since even if he had to work all evening, he needed to eat. Hopefully he was envisioning Chinese food, or pizza, or maybe something I'd cooked.

When I arrived a little earlier than planned, he raised his brow, greeted me with a kiss, and said he had to finish up.

"No rush. I'll get everything ready."

He glanced at the thermal bag in my hand and the messenger bag strapped across my chest. "Ready?"

"Don't worry about it. Go tie up your work and then we'll eat."

The raised brow made an appearance again, but he didn't argue. I kissed his cheek, then went to the kitchen. I paused a moment, listening for him to return to his office, before I started to unload. Not the food, which I'd leave for last to keep it warm, but I put down a fresh white tablecloth, set some candles—cheesy, I know—and then laid out his plates and silverware. I hopped over to the little stereo in his living room and slid in a CD of classical music, then turned it down low enough that it was barely audible. But it set the mood.

He caught me as I headed back to the kitchen, and drew me into his arms. "Oh, going fancy, I see."

"Yep." I wrapped my arms around him, reveling in the heat and strength he radiated. I doubted I'd ever get tired of that. "Go wash your hands and I'll have dinner ready."

"Wash my hands?"

"Yes." I leaned close so my lips brushed his ear. "I need a few seconds for the final prep, so get going."

He chuckled, kissed me, and stepped from my arms, his fingertips dragging down my back, over my hips, and away like a lingering goodbye. "Well, I've been told. Gotta go wash my hands."

He was smirking as he left. I dashed back into the kitchen, my heart suddenly racing. Quickly, I unloaded and plated the calamari appetizer, the stuffed mushrooms, and then our dinners: crab cake for him and herbed salmon for me. I thanked God and all that was holy that it was still piping hot. Then the last steps: I lit the candles and turned off the kitchen light, casting the table in their romantic glow—with the added bonus of hiding all the empty containers on the counter. Surveying my plan in action, I thought it looked good. A fancy dinner without leaving the house. Butterflies fluttered in my gut. Or did it look silly, like I was trying too hard?

"Isaac, why's the—" Logan turned the corner into the kitchen and saw what I'd prepared. "Oh."

I stood by the table, bowed, heart now pounding, and gestured at his seat. "Monsieur, if you would."

He stepped closer to me rather than the seat, and my heart made a bid for escaping up my throat. Didn't he like it? Then his lips sealed over mine in a slow, lingering kiss. He rested his hands on my waist and slid them to the top of my butt, holding me there as he deepened the kiss, the wet heat awakening a very different hunger before he pulled away. "Thank you."

"My pleasure."

"I meant for dinner."

A single laugh huffed out of my chest—a mixture of amusement and relief—spreading my lips in a wide smile. I bumped our noses together, the flickering candlelight making the action as intimate as a kiss. "It's all my pleasure, Logan. You've been working hard, and I wanted to . . . give you something nice."

Our grins matched as he bumped his nose back against mine. "You sure know how to encourage a guy to work hard."

We lingered a little longer, holding each other in the dark, but eventually my stomach called. "Come on, let's eat before it gets cold."

Once he'd sat, his eyes widened, taking in what I'd placed out—or else he couldn't see well in the dark, but it probably wasn't that. "Damn, everything looks good!"

"I'm glad you like it. I had to guess what you'd want tonight, but I couldn't imagine you turning down crab cakes from Être Nourri."

"It's fantastic." He reached across the table and folded his hand over mine, which was waiting not-so-patiently to pick up the fork and dig in. The food was wafting its alluring aroma, and as touching as our embrace had been a few minutes ago, I was getting hungry. But I still met his eyes and turned my hand to hold his. He smiled, pure as fucking gold. "Thank you."

I tried not to let my sappy smile take over, but I probably failed. "Happy Valentine's Day."

"Happy Valentine's Day." Then he finally took his hand back, plucked a stuffed mushroom from its little plate, and popped it into his mouth. He moaned in ridiculous delight. "Oh god, it's so good."

That led to several minutes of eating and voicing our complete satisfaction in a way that we couldn't do in the restaurant, at least not at the volume with which we did tonight. If words like *calamari* and *mushrooms* and *crab meat* weren't being thrown around, the neighbors would have thought we were having really good sex. As it was, they probably thought we were having really *weird* sex.

When the initial rush of savoring had taken place and we were both able to talk, I asked him how his day was.

"Not bad considering the runaround they've been giving me. I sent the 'finals'"—he included finger quotes—"this morning and did other projects while waiting for their reply." He exhaled, his shoulders sinking with the weight of the gust. "This dinner is the perfect way to relax. God, you're wonderful."

Heat flooded my cheeks, and I dropped my gaze to the lone piece of fried calamari remaining, before snatching it up. "Well, it was a bit self-serving, since I wanted to spend time with you. You have Emmett and Jackson to thank: they gave me the idea to bring Valentine's Day to you if you couldn't get away from work."

"Then I'll have to send them a bouquet of flowers. Though, wait. They're the ones with the baby? Maybe they'd prefer a bouquet of diapers instead."

I grinned at the image that painted. "Actually, I think they'd like to get a chance to meet you. It was hinted—" I raised my hand to show a small space between my forefinger and thumb "—a little, that it wasn't fair I'd met your friends and you hadn't met mine."

"Ooh, the vetting process."

"Or they want to steal you from me. I can't be sure which."

"Are the ones with the baby married? I doubt they want to steal me."

"Hey, maybe they're searching for a third. Possibly someone to help take care of Rosa."

Looking amused, Logan shook his head as he ate another bite of crab, then spent a moment with his eyes closed in bliss. When he opened them again, the teasing had faded. "I'd like to meet your friends too, you know. Any excuse to spend time with you."

My smile widened. "We'll have to set up a time, then. When everyone can make it. Not to overwhelm you or anything."

He chuckled. "You think I'd be overwhelmed so easily?"

I scoffed. "No. I just sometimes forget you don't flip out about things like I do."

"They're your friends—I trust that everything they do is in your best interest."

"Best interest in embarrassing me, more like," I mumbled.

"That works too."

I threw him the driest glare I could, but it was hard against the power of his smirk. It shouldn't be legal for a smirk to be that sexy. Especially when it was at my expense. And it shouldn't send a shiver through me. I distracted myself with the fantastic dinner, but the heat still sat deep in my chest, warming me as I talked about how my week had been, the concert I'd gone to with Roe, and the terrible direction a show Logan and I watched was heading. Exciting stuff.

And yet.

There was something magical about the night. Not only gazing across the candlelit table to meet his dark gaze. Not only sharing this splendid meal on this forced-romance consumer holiday. Not only getting to see each other after a long week of not. It was sharing all the little moments of our lives that the other hadn't been there for. Telling thrilling tales of misadventures at the grocery store. Yes, they were stupid and pointless, but by sharing them, we shared so much more. Like the threads of a shirt, a thousand tiny stories slowly weaved us closer and closer together.

A different kind of warmth blossomed in my chest and radiated through me. The smile on my lips was nearly bursting. I caught him staring at me and nearly blushed again. "What?"

"Nothing. That's a good look on you. I've missed seeing it this week."

And there was the blush, sweeping up my face full force. I didn't mind so much. "Well, once you're done that project and catch up, you can see it all you want."

"That is the best reward."

He was such a cheeseball and knew exactly how to make my blush intensify. But it was hard to be even slightly annoyed with him, because he segued seamlessly back into chatting about those silly, stupid things that had put the smile on my face in the first place.

After dinner, we both moved to the sink, dirty dishes in hand. After we set them down, I snagged him around the waist and tugged him to me, relishing the heat of his body after having gone so long without. I kissed him and tried not to sigh at the thought of letting him go. "Don't worry, I'll clean everything up. I know you have to go back to work, but I'm glad I could give you some time tonight not thinking about that stupid project."

His smile widened and he pulled me a little closer. Or maybe not *closer*, but he held me *firmer*. "Thank you. But now it's time for me to give you your Valentine's present."

"Oh?"

He squeezed where his hands were gripping my lower back. "I really was finishing up when you got here. The project's done, so you have me all evening. Oh, and there's a fruit tart from Paris Baguette in the fridge for us."

I leaned in, letting my words caress his ear. "Later. Once we've worked up an appetite."

"Oh, planning a trip to the gym? Sexy."

I slid my hands over his broad shoulders and gave them a squeeze. "Yeah, baby. We'll do some squats and thrusters and, uh, downward-facing dog . . ."

He muffled his snickers against my neck.

"You started it." I kissed the hinge of his jaw. "I was always more into aerobic exercise anyway."

"Gonna test my endurance?"

I nipped his earlobe. "And your flexibility."

"Oh?" I could hear the raised eyebrow that went with that. "Are you now?"

"Unless you don't want me to fuck you senseless?" I asked, all innocence.

He snorted a warm breath into the crook of my neck. "When have I ever not wanted that?"

"Usually when you're craving my delectable ass."

"Fair." He trailed kisses along my jaw and ended with a hot kiss. "Ready to go work out?"

I grinned, grabbed his hand, and pulled him into the bedroom.

CHAPTER SEVEN

The television screen cast white light over Roe's living room as the movie's closing lines called back to the opening, and then the end credits began to roll, bathing us in dark blue. I shifted, too comfortable in the cocoon of Logan's arms to want to get up and stretch like everyone else was doing. It wasn't a long movie, but we'd been caught up in the drama for the last half, and nobody had moved an inch.

Roe flicked on the lights, and a cry of disgruntled surprise rose up along with hands to block the brightness. I shouted and hid my face in the nook of Logan's arm, drowning myself in the heady depth of his scent: clean sweat from being packed in a small room with five other people, a hint of gasoline from where he'd filled up his tank, the lingering spice from his deodorant, worn thin this late in the day. I never wanted to leave.

"Wow," Logan said, his chest rumbling against my cheek, "that was a great movie. I can't believe I'd never heard of it."

"It flew under a lot of radars," Jenna said, releasing a grunt like she was stretching toward the ceiling.

"Which is a shame, because it's so good." Laura sighed. "Of course, it also empowers women and breaks the patriarchy, so I can't *imagine* why it didn't get more traction."

"Not to mention bringing attention to the natives of New Zealand and, well, not their plight, but kind of their living situation," Mark added.

"That's true," Logan said, "but beyond all that, it's a solid movie. Like, it hits these big goals, but it also entertains, has good acting and beautiful visuals. I mean, don't get me wrong, I enjoy political and socioeconomic depth as much as the next person—though the next person probably doesn't, but whatever. Anyway, I like those things, but sometimes the movies they're in are so dense that you can't enjoy the movie itself. So the message gets stifled by not being in an accessible medium. But if you can get the message across *while* entertaining? Perfect."

"Oh my god!" A second later Roe glomped Logan, which was awkward since I was still tucked against him, barely starting to peek out. All I saw as my eyes adjusted to the brightness was a flash of green, and then they were on top of us. "Thank you. That's exactly what I'm always saying. But Mark insists that we shouldn't dumb down the message simply to reach more people."

The hug lingered a little longer than I liked, but before I could pinch Roe's side and get them off, they leaped up and clapped their hands together. "So what should we watch next?"

I groaned and slowly unburrowed from my Logan-cave. "Can we take a break from movies, and chill? I'm visually exhausted."

Jenna stage-whispered, "And I heard Roe wanted to watch *Pan's Labyrinth.*"

"I definitely need a break before that!" I rolled over and sat up, Logan's arm still wrapped around my shoulders, but like what you'd see in any park.

Logan squeezed my arm. "What's wrong with *Pan's Labyrinth?*"

"Nothing. But this film put us through an emotional wringer, and I'm so not ready for subtitles and woman's disease."

Laura leaned over and smacked my shoulder.

"Ow! Hey! I only mean it's a depressing movie!"

She paused, hand raised for a second smack, then lowered it and shrugged. "Yeah, it is."

I shifted in Logan's arm and glanced around at my friends. It was a shame Jackson and Emmett hadn't been able to make it, but getting a babysitter for a movie night wasn't worth it. Sometimes we'd take it to their place, but the kid had been crankier than usual today, and they'd requested to sit this one out. "Has anyone heard the weather forecast for this weekend?"

"Why, want to get snowed in?" Mark waggled his bushy red eyebrows in the most ridiculous manner, in case we didn't get the gist.

"Need to stock up on eggs, milk, and bread first," Logan said.

"Oooh, gonna make me French toast?" I teased, but as soon as the idea was out there, it was appealing.

"You were the one asking about the weather. I thought you were going to make it for me."

"Well, no one actually said if we were getting any snow." I glanced around. Roe already had their phone out.

"Two to three inches on Sunday, but nothing that would trap you inside. Unless, of course, you want to be trapped inside."

"Two to three inches sounds like a good time for French toast."

Mark whispered, "That's a super weird euphemism."

I snickered. "Oh, trust me, Mark, it's way bigger than three inches."

As everyone had a chuckle, Logan's cheeks darkened, so I kissed one of them. "And he knows how to use it."

Logan turned and caught my mouth in a quick peck. "You're terrible."

"They bring out the worst in me."

"Mostly Mark," Roe interjected. "He only has sex on the brain."

"'Cause I'm carrying your portion. Someone had to take it!"

Roe grabbed a pillow off the couch and swung it; Mark leaped up with a pillow in his hands to block the strike.

I watched for a moment, then focused on Logan as the two of them had their pillow fight. "So, what do you think of my friends?"

"Pretty sure they can hear us." Logan squeezed my shoulders. "They're a lot like you, so a good bunch. Though you're the most handsome."

I laughed and kissed his chin. "Well played."

"Roe," Jenna whined, "they're being cute again. Make it stop."

Roe paused in the middle of pummeling Mark and glanced over their shoulder. "Why is that my job? As long as they aren't fucking on my couch, I don't care."

"Note: no fucking on Roe's couch," Logan said. "Wait, does that mean we can fuck—"

"No." Roe's flat tone left no room for argument, not that I thought Logan had had actual plans to fuck anywhere in Roe's house.

"Darn."

I shook my head and dragged the conversation back to my original idea. "So Saturday is gonna be nice?"

Roe snorted. "If three-degree temps are 'nice,' then sure. Oh, and twenty-mile-per-hour winds."

"That won't be a problem. Wasn't exactly planning on hiking or anything," I said.

"Yeah? And what were you planning?"

"To go visit Jackson and Emmett if they're free." I looked to Logan. "If you'd like to meet them tomorrow?"

"I'm totally up for that."

"Wow. Making plans right in front of us. Rude," Laura muttered.

I glanced at her. "Well, I was going to invite you all to join us, but I changed my mind, now."

Jenna elbowed her girlfriend. "We have plans anyway, remember?"

"Oh yeah. Your family is such a pai—"

"Payload of delight?"

"Yes. A giant payload of delight."

Jenna grinned. "Mom's making her apple coffee cakes."

Laura's eyes lit up. "All is forgiven."

Beside me, Logan tensed, and I stretched my arm across his torso to give him a comforting squeeze. Mentions of family didn't always bother him, but sometimes the small things hurt the most—because they were the most unexpected. Like papercuts under a fingernail.

"So you guys are all out to your families?" Logan asked, and I had to reassess my conclusion on why he'd tensed.

"I am," Jenna said. "Laura is to her immediate family, and they're . . . coping still."

Laura made a face, scrunching her freckled nose. "My extended family is pretty conservative, so we're not rushing to tell them. Plus I never see them except at the yearly family reunion that I want to get out of anyway."

Mark nodded. "And my parents told me when I was ten that if I was gay or straight or whatever, it was 'fine by them' and they'd always love me. So it wasn't so much coming out to them as it was telling them who I was dating."

Roe shrugged. "My parents are hella confused and don't get it, but yeah, I'm out."

Logan's arm tightened around my shoulders, and suddenly it felt constrictive, not supportive. But he didn't question why I wasn't out to mine when everyone else was. Maybe he knew it was none of his damn business. Maybe he knew I wasn't ready for the fallout that seemed almost inevitable.

"What about you?" Mark asked, and for a moment I thought he was asking *me*, like he didn't know.

"My parents knew, but my grandparents passed early, and my aunt and uncle were mostly estranged from us." Logan's shrug was a taut jerk. "Now it's just me."

"Oh." Mark winced. "Sorry."

Another tight shrug.

"So," I said, overly loud, "if people want to invite themselves over to Jackson's tomorrow, I'll let you know if we're going." In fact, I pulled out my phone and shot off a text to the Jackson and Emmett chat thread.

A few minutes—and a conversation switch—later, and Jackson replied.

We're free. If you come over for lunch, afterward we can put Rosa down for her nap and actually converse like adults.

I grinned. *Sounds good. Mark and Roe might "stop by" too.*

Okay. They going to bring eye candy too?

I glanced up at them and interrupted, "Hey, Jackson wants to know if you two are bringing eye candy tomorrow."

"If I had any," Mark grumbled.

"Skittles?" Roe offered, gray eyes lit with teasing.

I wouldn't expect much from them, I texted.

When I slid my phone back into my pocket, Logan said, "So I'm eye candy, now, am I?"

I gave him a dry glare. "My sister seems to think so."

He grinned. "I'm never going to live that down, am I?"

"It does have the makings of a sitcom. But I'm glad she brought you." I tried for a sultry leer, but it was probably more sap than sult.

"So am I," he whispered, and closed the distance to kiss me.

It was soft and sweet, and the voices around us faded to a murmur that hummed indistinctly through my body. I couldn't pay attention to that insignificant buzz when Logan's fingers were trailing electricity along my neck. He cupped the back, but he didn't pull me forward. Just held me there. Maybe he remembered that we were in a room full of people—one of us should—or maybe he wanted to tease my lips with his tongue and keep me from diving in for more.

He drew back slowly, and when I opened my eyes, his met mine. They seemed darker, deeper, than ever before. They made promises—not only the ones that would be fulfilled later tonight in bed, but ones beyond that, into tomorrow and the weeks to come. We hadn't said the words, but in his eyes I saw them: *I love you*.

I wanted to whisper them back, but here among my friends in this absolutely ordinary moment didn't seem the right time. So I tilted my lips and held his gaze as I brushed a kiss against his mouth. I hoped he could read the same words in my eyes.

"So are we ready for another movie?" Roe's voice broke through the moment.

I blinked and glanced over to them. Then to the clock on the wall. "Um, maybe we could order dinner first?"

When I checked back, Roe had their neatly sculpted brow raised, silently chiding me for getting lost in Logan. But they didn't say anything about it. "Sounds good. What are folks in the mood for?"

Everyone broke out in discussion, and I turned to Logan.

He was staring at me, his devilish grin gone. He looked besotted. I leaned my head on his shoulder and tilted my face so I could still sort of see him. "So, what are you in the mood for?"

A deep chuckle vibrated his chest, and the sweetness melted back to sexiness. "I think Roe already said I couldn't have that until later."

The kiss was awkward with how our heads were positioned, but that made it more fun. "Fine, then, what do you want to eat?"

Another chuckle, and I didn't even need him to say something. "For dinner," I added.

"Pizza's good for me," he said, loud enough for the group to hear. I grinned. "Yeah, it'll do for now."

Within twenty minutes of arriving at Jackson and Emmett's the next day, Logan had his hands full of Rosa while I helped Jackson with the dishes and Emmett made another sippy cup for her.

"Sorry," I said, although Logan didn't seem at all bothered by the whimpering child. "I didn't expect we'd get here and be put to work."

Logan laughed. "Hey, I've got no siblings, so this is the closest I've been to being an uncle so far. My friends need to get on the ball."

Jackson smiled, all innocence. "Maybe they're waiting for you to start them off."

I glared at him.

"Oh please," Logan said, seemingly oblivious to the looks I was casting. "Not that you have to get hitched before having a kid, but it sure does make it easier to have an extra set of hands around. And until recently it was only me."

I cleared my throat. "Do you want kids?"

He must have heard the reluctance in my voice, because he brought Rosa to stand beside me where I was drying a pot. "I could take them or leave them. I'm a little sad that my family will pretty much be dying out if I don't, but I do admit being the uncle has a lot more appeal."

"That's . . . good to hear."

He bumped my shoulder with his. "Not into kids?"

"Oh, I love *other people's* kids. Rosa is a delight. Because I give her back and go home. I . . . I don't want to do it. I don't want to fu—um, mess up and I don't want them to hate me and I don't want to be a bad parent." I sighed. "It sounds stupid."

"No!" Rosa shouted.

It was pretty much the only word in her vocabulary at the moment. The shout was probably because Logan had shifted her to his other arm and she was cranky. But the timing made me smile.

"Like this wise little child said," Logan said once we'd all stopped being stupidly awed by her, "there's no bad reason to *not* want a kid. Maybe if we were in the zombie apocalypse—or, well, any apocalypse, I guess—but there are plenty of kids and parents to go around as it is. Reluctant parents are not going to make good parents."

I smirked. "I think you implied I'd be a bad parent."

He rolled his eyes. "But a great uncle."

Emmett arrived and took Rosa and her sippy cup to the table, and Jackson and I finished the dishes. Eventually we all migrated to the table with father and daughter.

"So," Jackson said to Logan, "I'm totally not going to point out that it's been like two months and we're only meeting you now."

"Oh my god," I groaned, although this had definitely been expected.

Logan smiled, like Jackson was teasing. Maybe Jackson was. I never could be sure. "I apologize profusely. The one downside of working for yourself is you're the only person to get a job done. I do hope Isaac told you this and didn't let you think that I didn't want to meet everyone."

"I did," I said. "He's being a bastard."

"Language," Emmett reminded, the hypocritical so-and-so.

"He's being a disgruntled illegitimate child," I amended.

Jackson sighed, as if I were a burden he had to put up with. "I'm glad we finally got to meet you. You seem to make Isaac happy." He thumped his fist into his left hand, which probably would have seemed more threatening coming from Emmett, but I wasn't going to tell him. "Make sure you don't hurt him."

"I have no intention of doing that."

"Is my virtue safe now?" I grumbled.

"Oh, something tells me your virtue has long since been marred."

Logan smirked, and I smacked him. "Virtue besmircher."

"You loved it."

The warmth flooded my chest, much like it had the night before when I'd first wanted to whisper those three words. Who cared if the moment wasn't special and romantic? I leaned close, lips brushing his ear as I said, "Because I love you."

He turned, his lips meeting mine in a kiss as he whispered back, "I love you too."

My friends had the decency to not call us on being disgustingly cute and fussed with Rosa instead. I couldn't remember if we'd afforded them the same courtesy when they'd been in the new-love stage.

"Well," Jackson said, "I'm glad you finally got to meet Isaac's family."

I stiffened, and Jackson must have seen it, because he added, "His chosen family, that is. The most important kind."

"Absolutely." Logan slid an arm around my shoulders as if nothing awkward had passed across the table. "I'm sorry it took so long."

"Meeting the family is a big step."

"Yeah," Emmett scoffed, "next comes the marriage proposal."

"Hey! It's been *two* months! And I barely got to see him for most of that," I said.

Logan smiled. "Don't worry, babe, I always figured I'd propose on the one-year anniversary of us meeting."

"Does that mean on Christmas Day or the day after?"

"I guess that'll be the surprise." He gave me a cheeky grin, and I knew he was joking. Hell, many relationships didn't last a year. Who knew where we'd be.

I rolled my eyes and kissed his cheek. "Dork."

Jackson and Emmett launched into the standard questions when meeting a new friend: his job, his interests, his favorite anime.

"Oh god," Logan said, "you're all giant nerds."

"Pot, kettle," I reminded him.

"I wasn't judging! I was excited. My friends are kind of nerds, but nothing like you guys. I always feel like a dweeb when I'm with them and arguing about inconsistencies in the Star Wars universe."

It was hard to imagine Logan—broad-shouldered, rippling-muscles Logan—calling himself a dweeb, but I had long since come to accept and delight in his nerdiness, whether it was reading queer romance novels or spending a weekend rewatching the director's cut of *Lord of the Rings*.

"You do not give the dweeb first impression," Emmett assured, and they shared a fist bump like two dude-bros would do, which was fitting since Emmett and Logan could totally pass as them. And yet here they were bonding over being giant—literally—nerds.

Then Rosa threw her peas in the way toddlers do, and we were all directed back to more messy matters.

CHAPTER EIGHT

Spring was a tricky thing that was made of lies. Supposedly March twentieth was spring, but most years it was cold and rainy, which wasn't a great welcome for the season. This year had the dubious benefit of heralding in Easter shortly after, which I didn't give two fucks about, but which my mother had *insisted* I come home to celebrate with her and Dad.

"Honey," she whined into the phone while I chopped up a head of broccoli for dinner. I wanted dinner and this conversation to be done by the time Logan got here, and I definitely had higher hopes for the former.

"Mom, I love to see you guys"—I only sort of stretched the truth to breaking—"but now's not a great time."

"Your sister's coming."

Which was the only reason what I'd said hadn't been a total lie. "I know."

I was a little curious about what trickery Mom had used to get Sue to agree to that again. Maybe she was just a better offspring.

"And I'm sure she'd like her brother there," Mom said, "after the recent breakup with her boyfriend."

I almost bit my tongue in surprise, thinking of her with Logan at Christmas. But then I remembered that Sue had "broken up" with Logan back in January and had been dating someone else since then. A friend of a friend of Logan who he'd helpfully hooked her up with. As far as I knew from Logan's reports, the breakup had been amicable and she was staying friends with the guy. Nothing necessitating brotherly support. "She seemed okay when I talked to her."

"Oh, so you call her and not your mother?"

I should have seen that coming. Thankfully I could say, "She called me." She *had*. After I texted that she should call me when she had a minute.

"You should make an effort to stay connected with your family. We're the only one you've got."

I sighed. She must have heard my fight weakening, because she went on. "And your father and I won't be around forever."

"You're both in good health and young." But thinking about Logan and his parents, already taken from him by a car crash, tripled the guilt Mom was so good at brewing. I wasn't appreciating what I had while I had it. Logan would give almost anything to have more time with his parents, and here I was doing everything I could to get out of going to see mine. "But I sure do miss your Easter ham."

"Oh you! We sure will be happy to see you."

"It'll be good to see you too." I hoped my sigh didn't carry over the line. "What time do you want me to be there?"

It turned out phone calls didn't take nearly as long when I gave in to all her demands. Five minutes later I was off the phone, tied in to spend Easter Sunday with my folks and bring a lemon meringue pie. Least there would be good food and Sue. On the other hand, it meant that I'd be leaving behind Logan.

No matter what I chose, I'd be left with an unhealthy dose of guilt.

I turned my attention to preparing dinner and tried not to think about breaking the news to him. Chop, sauté, mix, batter, season, bake. A dozen or so ingredients that came together beautifully, if I did say so myself.

Even over the banging of pans, the hum of the exhaust fan, and my own humming—a habit I'd picked up from my mother—I heard the *snick* of the key turning in the lock. Despite my worries, my body went taut with excitement, a breath caught in my chest, and a smile curled into my cheeks.

"Honey, I'm home," Logan announced, stepping into the kitchen. He spread his arms wide and let me give him a good once-over. His cornflower-blue T-shirt tracked the curves of his muscles, clinging to his biceps and revealing the art down his arms. He was wearing his heavy jeans and boots, and as I stepped into his arms, I could smell the lingering scent of exhaust. I buried my nose in his neck and inhaled, pushing past that caustic odor to Logan's.

"Welcome home. You rode your bike."

His hum rumbled against my mouth as I worked my kisses up his shoulder and neck. "You can tell?"

"You only wear those boots when you ride. Also, you stink like city when you do."

His arms slid around me, and he tucked his hands into my back pockets. "And yet you're sniffing me like a tom on the prowl."

"Maybe I really like those boots." I dragged my hands up his sides, playing over the spots I knew were a little ticklish, then swooped them around his back to hook them on his shoulders. "Also, I'm looking forward to when it's warm enough that I can ride with you. Which is not today."

"No." He sniffed. "Today smells like something delicious."

"Shit." I pulled away and dashed over to the sauce that wasn't yet burning on the stove. "Dinner will be ready in a bit."

"Mmm." He stepped behind me, hands on my hips and crotch on my ass, like he wanted me to burn dinner. "I'm definitely hungry."

I wiggled my hips in time with the stirring and tried not to giggle as I said, "Good, because I've got plenty for you to eat."

He nestled his lips against my neck, his warm breath brushing my skin like the barest of kisses. "You never leave me unsatisfied."

"Ohh, someone knows what to say to get lucky," I teased.

His answer was soft and low, suddenly serious. "I don't have to get lucky—I already am."

The kiss on my neck finished the line: *because I have you.*

I melted like the butterscotch sap I was. "I love you."

He gave a playful nip on my shoulder, then straightened, simply holding me close, his head beside mine. "I love you too."

We danced around the kitchen a little more as I put the final touches on dinner, and despite all the potential distractions, it managed to reach the table unburned.

"How was your day?" I asked, feeling like a housewife, even though I, too, had been at work all day.

He shrugged. "Same old. Lug International wants me to design a new logo for them, so that's exciting." He chuckled. "Well, as exciting as logo design ever is."

"But it's a big name, so that's huge! I'm surprised they're going with a freelancer. Don't they have a whole staff that does that for them?"

"Yeah, but they wanted 'fresh blood' to bring 'new ideas' to the table. I did some work for one of the suits, it seems, and she was impressed enough to recommend me. Voilà."

"That's awesome!"

"We'll see. How was your day? Big boss still being a fuck-face?" His lips curled in a slight smirk, as if he was concerned but also a bit amused at my struggle. I wanted to kiss that smirk right off him.

I groaned instead. "I don't know. He gave his directive and then left for vacation. The mini-bosses are all trying to figure out a way to implement it without fucking everyone over, which is nice of them. Of course, that means we're being called into meetings every ten minutes with 'Will this work?' being thrown at us." I sighed, letting my frustration escape with the air. "We think we have a solution and it'll be okay. So that's what we'll be implementing this week."

"Least it's a short one? And you get a long weekend? Isn't your company off Friday and Monday? I'm sure we can find something to do to make up for a shitty week."

"Yeah." I grimaced. I'd been hoping to put the conversation off until later—to avoid spoiling what had turned out to be a pretty excellent meal—but there was no way to change the subject without being obvious. Or lying. "My mom wants me to go there for Easter, though." I dropped my eyes to my plate and focused on cutting the chicken. "So we won't be able to spend the whole weekend together."

There was a definite pause then, and I was too much of a coward to face him. I didn't want to see the disappointment at not being able to spend the time together, although he'd probably understand. He knew how important family was. And he knew I'd rather spend the time with him than my parents.

When the silence stretched on, I finally forced my gaze up. Logan was staring at me, his thick brow pulled low and taut, his lips a tense line across his face. He looked disappointed, yeah; he also looked hurt. Was it because I was leaving him all alone on the holiday? Neither of us were religious, so I hadn't thought it would be a big deal. Not like

Christmas or something. I mean, I knew lots of people who didn't get together with their family at all on Easter.

He set down his fork and knife, his eyes still piercing into mine. "So you're going to your parents'?"

The way he said it was too flat, too crisp to be a casual confirmation. It screamed *This is leading to a trap*. I licked my lips, holding his gaze, and had to swallow once before I managed to say, "Yes. I don't want to, but yeah, Mom talked me into it."

"Alone?"

Suddenly the tension running across his shoulders and straightening his back took on a different meaning. He wasn't upset that I was going to be gone for one day; he was upset I was leaving him behind.

Shit.

I drew in a shaky breath. "That was the plan." My voice quivered and nearly broke. I didn't know what I was more scared of: the disappointment I knew would keep happening or that he'd ask—

"You don't want me to come with you?"

That.

He had to know how badly I wanted him to come with me. To *have* him with me. To be able to show him off to my parents as my awesome boyfriend and get my mom off my back. But . . .

"You can't." I winced. That wasn't how I'd meant it to come out.

"I can't." His cold repetition of my words made it clear that verbal comprehension wasn't what he was struggling with. "Just like that. 'You can't.'"

Shit. "I . . ."

He waited as I floundered. Panic swelled in my chest, tightening my lungs and turning my stomach into a knot of iron.

"I . . ." I made myself swallow, trying to loosen my tongue and throat so I could speak. "I want you to come with me, but you can't." I winced again. At least this time he didn't say anything. Gave me a chance to try to save myself. "I'm not ready. It's too soon."

Jesus fuck, could I use any more clichés? He didn't look too impressed with them either. "So what you said before wasn't true?" He must have read my confusion on my face, because he added, "When we met for coffee that first day. After Christmas. You said if you had someone serious, someone you wanted to take home, then you'd tell them."

The knot in my stomach bloated and rolled over like a beached whale. "That's still true."

The lines in his face hardened, not like he was angrier, but like his mask had become brittle. "So I'm not that serious?"

"I . . ." *Shit.* "It's complicated."

"Complicated," he repeated in that flat tone again. Not good.

"Fuck. Logan." I pushed aside my plate and slid my hands across the table, palms up, begging him to take them. He didn't, but I didn't back down either. "I want to. It's been so long. But they're my parents, and the part of me that says 'You're serious about Logan, tell them' is fighting with 'It's only been three months' and *I'm not ready.*"

My voice cracked with a whimper, and I had to lower my eyes in shame and guilt. Because I was a coward, and that was all it was. I was a coward and feared my parents' rejection more than his love could compensate for and he would see that and he'd know what a loser I was and he'd walk away and I'd lose him and—

His hands slid into mine. My gaze jerked up to him.

His smile was drenched in so much pain that it hurt to see. "Okay."

"Okay?"

He curled his fingers with mine, his grip tight and only a little shaky. "Yeah. I get it. They're your parents. It's hard."

"I love them. And I love you. I . . ." I was a coward who couldn't face losing them because of who I was.

"You're not ready." He lifted my hands to his lips and kissed a knuckle on each side. "I understand."

"Thank you. It's—" I choked out a wet laugh. "Fuck, it's not you. I'm *proud* of dating you. You're amazing. I just want to delay the inevitable fallout."

"You don't know it's inevitable." He squeezed my hands. "I'm not saying you need to tell them now, but maybe give them a chance. They almost seemed to cope with having Sue dating *a brown person.*" He said the last bit with a mocking gasp and joined it with an eye roll.

It was my turn to squeeze his hands. "Yeah. But now they'd be dealing with their suddenly gay son dating a suddenly gay brown person." My smile wobbled. "I'm sorry. You shouldn't have to put up with my shit or theirs. You picked a bad boyfriend."

He tugged my hands. "Get over here."

I let go of him so I could circle the table, and he pulled me onto his lap. I wasn't tiny, but his muscular thighs held me like I was nothing, and his large arms around me were fucking magical. Like a shield against all the shit in the world. I rested my head on his shoulder and sighed, and he tightened his arms, holding me close.

"I didn't pick a bad boyfriend. I fell in love with a guy with baggage. We've all got it."

"You don't," I mumbled against his neck. "You're perfect."

He kissed the corner of my jaw. "I'll remind you of that when you get pissed about me leaving my clothes on the floor."

"Not just on the floor," I couldn't help prodding, "but *right next to the hamper.*"

His laugh shook both of us, jostling out the tension. "See, I'm not perfect. And I've got baggage too. A wise person once told me that love is accepting all of someone. We'll work through this."

I wrapped my arms around his neck and held on tight. "Thank you. I love you. Please never doubt that."

He nudged my cheek with his chin until I raised my head, and then he kissed me. "I love you too."

Part of me noticed he didn't agree to never doubting it, but I wasn't about to look a gift horse in the mouth. I had him, and I had a reprieve from having to tell my parents.

Unfortunately, that reprieve didn't get me out of *visiting* my parents. Logan kept me company for the trip down—only as a voice floating out of my speakers, but he helped pass the time. It was stupidly hard to say goodbye once I'd parked the car. Eventually we did, though, since my sister was already here and I couldn't sit in the driveway all day. I'd get in trouble with my parents, and the lost day away from Logan would be wasted.

So I grabbed the pie and headed inside. Everyone was in the kitchen: my dad over a plate of eggs and sausage, my mom bustling to get the ham ready, and my sister leaning against the counter, out of Mom's way.

In greeting, Mom said, "Take your shoes off."

I glanced down at my socked feet. "Um, done. You have room in the fridge for the pie?"

She sighed and spun around, reaching to take the pie from my hands, but I stepped back. "No, you're busy, I can put it in. Just wanted to make sure there was room."

Turning back to the ham, she said, "If you open the door, you'll find out." I could practically hear the eye roll.

"Right . . ."

I shared a look with Sue, who shrugged and mouthed, *She's in a mood*. At least, I thought that was what she said.

There was room in the fridge, an almost perfect pie-shaped space, actually. I put the pie in, wondering why Mom couldn't have simply said yes. But, hey, that was Mom. "How is everybody?"

"Your father's back has been acting up, so I had to do the weeding—did you see the daffodils are blooming rather lovely in the front garden?—and the next morning my back hurt so badly, I thought both of us were going to be bed-ridden! And then where would we be with you two living so far away? We'd have to call the ambulance, is what we'd have to do, or wait hours for one of you, and wouldn't that be something?"

She didn't pause for breath—not even pretending that she wanted replies. "But eventually your father was able to get up, and once he fetched me some Tylenol and a heating pad, I was able to get up on my own. Crisis averted!"

"I'm glad you both were okay. You should be more careful weeding, Mom; you know how tough it is on you." I glanced at my dad, who was still focused on the Sunday paper and his breakfast. "Dad, did you go to the doctor about your back?"

He grunted.

"No, he hasn't," Mom answered. "I told him to go as soon as it started acting up, but did he listen? Nope. And then he couldn't get out of bed until he took drugs, and that's no way to be. I suggested he go to my chiropractor—you know he's worked miracles with my pain—but I'd be better off talking to a wall."

"I'm not going to that quack," Dad grumbled. "My back's fine."

"If you were stuck in bed, that doesn't sound fine," Sue chimed in.

"You a doctor now?" Dad said.

"Common sense says pain that interrupts your life means you're not fine," I said before Sue could say whatever scathing answer was on her tongue. Judging by her expression, it wouldn't have calmed the situation any.

Dad grunted again. "It was just a bit sore. Your mother's throwing it out of proportion."

"Well, if it keeps bothering you, you should go to the doctor. Weren't you always saying 'better safe than sorry'?" My advice would fall on deaf ears, but I couldn't *not* say something.

"Sure, sure, if it's a bother, I will."

Aka, he wasn't going to the doctor.

I turned to my sister. "So, Sue, how are you?"

She grinned at me, as if my desperate ploy to change the topic was a little too obvious. "Heartbroken if you ask Mom."

"Honey, you don't need to joke about your pain. It's tough to be dumped. Grieving after having your heart broken is a natural process."

Sue rolled her eyes at me, as if silently saying, *See what I mean?* "Mom, I'm not heartbroken. It was a pretty mutual breakup. We're still friends."

"Of course, dear." Mom didn't believe in men and women being friends, not really. They either dated or were married or they were the friends of the partner/spouse.

I could feel the heavy-duty sigh that Sue was repressing, and wasn't sure if I wanted to laugh or beat my head against the wall. Interference seemed the best bet. "Well, now you're free to pursue whoever you want. A good rich man."

She smirked. "With broad shoulders and bulging biceps and his own company."

I threw her a glare, but it only made her smirk widen.

"That certainly sounds like a nice prospect," Mom said, a little too breathlessly for my tastes. Especially knowing that Sue had been referring to Logan.

"Yeah." Sue winked at me, and thankfully our parents were too distracted to notice. "Too bad all the good ones are gay or taken."

Mom tutted. "Now, now, don't forget your brother's still single."

This would have been a perfect time to mention that I was taken and gay, then watch the chips fall where they would. Sue even left me a few moments to speak up. When I didn't, she took the opening.

"Yeah, but he's not a good one, is he?"

"Well not for you! He's your brother." Mom giggled.

It wasn't clear if she was oblivious or being willfully ignorant to the insult aimed at me. My dad grunted and shook the paper—his only addition to the conversation. I debated asking him about his latest home-improvement project, but that would probably cause a fight with Mom.

"So did you guys color eggs this year?" I asked in a rather desperate attempt to change the subject.

"I thought we could do that as a fun activity while you and Sue were here."

Are you fucking kidding me? "Uh, that's . . . a thing to do."

Sue rolled her eyes so hard I prepared to catch them. "Mom, is that really necessary?"

"Your father loves his hard-boiled eggs, and I didn't want to have to make them alone again this year—"

"Doesn't Dad help?" What I meant was *Dad should help if he wants the damn eggs.*

"Oh, it's such a bother to him. But we can sit around and chat while we do it, and it'll be fun."

"So we're going to make a dozen eggs and paint them just so Dad can eat them?" Sue asked.

"Yep." Mom shut the oven door as if closing the matter, and I supposed she had. We could refuse to help her, but then we'd be bad children and she would never let us forget it. We would be dragged into coloring eggs much like we'd been dragged here. Because she was our mother and we loved her.

I shared a glance with Sue, shrugged in defeat, and once again changed the subject. "How's your garden, Mom?"

Thankfully that was a safe subject and carried us on to other safe subjects, like movies we'd seen recently—none with guys kissing, so Mom couldn't complain—books we were reading, and Sue's new knitting hobby, which made Mom unreasonably excited.

But the topics weren't boyfriends, girlfriends, or babies, so it was a win.

The egg coloring after dinner wasn't that bad. Mom realized at the last minute that she didn't actually have the vinegar or the food dyes, so we broke out an old box of crayons and drew on the eggs, cursing all the while that we hadn't let them cool down enough. Sue and I slipped in a few inside jokes that Mom and Dad would never get—or we hoped they wouldn't.

Sue and I were still laughing as we cartoned up the eggs and washed the waxy residue off our hands. Shoulder to shoulder, we fought over the small sink like we were still kids. It felt good—this was why I came home. I bumped against her, my cheeks hurting with my grin. "Logan says hi."

She bumped me back. "Boyfriend stealer."

"You're just jealous."

She sighed in a swoon-like manner and rested her head on my shoulder. "I am a little. You seem happy with him."

"I am." I dropped my voice, paranoid my parents might hear us. "I love him, you know?"

"I got the feeling." She reached up on tiptoe and kissed my cheek. "I'm happy for you."

"Thanks. I'm glad someone is."

"Who—"

"What are you two doing in there taking so long?" my mom called, peeking into the already cramped space. "Come on, we've still got pie to eat!"

We followed her out, the conversation dropped in favor of the more enjoyable option: eating pie.

That night, I got home later than I'd planned. It would have been nice to be welcomed back by Logan with a kiss and a hug. To fall into bed together and wake up together. But I was going over to his place in the morning and spending the day with him, so there was that. Even if it wasn't enough.

CHAPTER NINE

"April showers bring May flowers," Alessa said, spreading out a blanket over the soft grass in the park where Logan and I and his friends were enjoying the first really nice weekend.

"But what do May flowers bring?" Matti asked.

I groaned, prepared for the bad pun—and yes, I realized the hypocrisy.

"Allergies," Troy mumbled through a stuffy nose. "Whose idea was this?"

"Did you take your antihistamines or whatever?" Bryan asked.

"No."

"Do you complain about this every year?"

"Yes."

Bryan let out an aggravated sigh, and Alessa continued, "I apologize to those among us with allergies—"

"Aka, me," Troy grumbled.

"—but as per our annual May Day celebration—"

"Which should have been three weeks ago," Logan pointed out.

"—that has been delayed because of rain," Alessa added, a hint of annoyance coloring her tone. She paused, glancing around as if daring anyone else to interrupt. "We are here on this May Day celebration to welcome spring!"

"Halle-fucking-lujah!" Erika raised a bottle of grape juice that looked suspiciously not like Welch's. "And we're having perfect weather. *Finally*," she muttered under her breath.

I was grateful for the weather, and not just because I was getting stir-crazy. Today I would finally be getting on Logan's bike. We'd had to come separately—I'd taken the bus—but after the picnic, I would get to ride it with him. Not that I'd been anxiously waiting for this since December.

Oh sure, I could have gone one of the dozen times he rode it over the winter, but it had been cold and my desire to ride was not enough to cancel out the biting winds the bike would have exposed me to. Despite all his fancy gear, he'd been frozen solid after a few of those trips.

But today was warm and sunny, and as I slid my arm around his waist, I knew it was going to be a good day.

We'd set up near a tree, where we could escape to for shade when the May sun got too intense for our sun-starved flesh. I was a little jealous of Erika and Jacob, who with their darker skin, still needed to apply sunscreen but wouldn't likely turn into neon-pink otters. Even Logan, Alessa, and Matti were likely to be spared.

Bryan and Troy met my eyes as we all pulled out bottles of sunscreen, and we shared a rueful grin as we started lathering up.

"Need me to get your back?" Logan offered, kneeling behind me.

I glanced down at my shirt—yep, still wearing it—and then over my shoulder at him. His eyes sparkled in the sunlight, his smile broad and carefree. He was fucking beautiful. "Uh?"

In the wide-open space, his laugh seemed bigger somehow, like he'd kept it bottled up all winter. "Okay, okay. I could do your neck. Or—" he swiped at my nose, and I felt the lotion smear "—make sure your face is clear."

"Sure, but . . ." I batted my eyes in the most ridiculous manner I could think of and pitched my voice as high as it would go. "Be gentle."

He shuffled around in front of me—which was as graceful as it sounds—and resumed kneeling there. He cupped my jaw, caressing his thumb along my cheek and picking up the conversation as if the position change hadn't happened. "Certainly. You're too precious to break."

A handful of grass flew at us—and fell short. "Get a room!"

Logan playfully leered at Troy. "That's later."

"Great," Troy grumbled, "now I'm congested, stinking of sunscreen and have a hard-on."

Logan picked up one of the dandelions that had nearly reached us and threw it about as effectively back at Troy. "Stop perving on my boyfriend."

Troy did an impressive eyebrow wiggle. "How do you know it's him I'm perving on?"

Before Logan could answer, I leaped forward and hugged him possessively to my chest, glaring at Troy. "No. Mine. Get your own!"

"Oh! A challenge."

"Careful," Alessa chimed in, "or he'll take on both of you."

"Take that as you will," Erika added.

"Oh hush," Troy said, giving Alessa the stink-eye. Then he looked back at me with a friendly leer. "Don't worry, your boyfriend is safe from me."

I rolled my eyes and sat back. "Good to know."

Logan shook his head and rubbed in the rest of the sunscreen I'd missed on my forehead, cheeks, and nose—pretty much all of it, it seemed—and the conversation around us moved on to what foods and games people had brought. I soon learned Erika had absolutely, definitely, totally not brought wine in the Welch's bottle, wink-wink, nudge-nudge.

Snacks and drinks were dug out and consumed, and then a Frisbee appeared and I was dragged from my comfortable resting spot against Logan's shoulder to join some incarnation of Frisbee, football, and keep-away that mostly served to make me hoarse from yelling, and sweaty.

By the time we collapsed—well, I collapsed; everyone else seemed more fit, the bastards—onto our blankets, it was time for lunch and reapplication of sunscreen. Thankfully there was plenty of both.

"You're not too bad at Frisbee." Bryan patted my back, plastering my sweaty shirt to my sweaty skin. Ew. "Though, it would help if you threw the disk to your teammates."

I chuckled, only a little uncomfortably. "I wasn't actually sure who was on my team most of the time."

"We chose sides!" Troy shouted from where he was dishing out salad.

"But whenever I gave it to my teammate, people yelled at me!"

"That's because you were breaking the rules," Bryan said.

I didn't know the rules! I wanted to scream, but shrugged instead. "Sorry."

"No worries. We'll give your team a handicap next time."

"I thought I was the handicap," I said, only half-joking.

"You said it!" Alessa crowed, and everyone broke into laughter, except Logan and Erika, who seemed to be in deep contemplation over a tub of pasta salad.

I had never bragged about my made-up-sports skills, so they didn't need to rag me so hard. Maybe they didn't like me. Or maybe this was how they were with each other? It seemed kind of harsh though. Not how I'd welcome someone to a group. Maybe this was their not-so-subtle way to tell me I wasn't welcome? Had I done something to annoy them?

With an awkward shrug, I hid my discomfort beneath a smile and started handing out plates and plasticware, then settled next to Logan, ostensibly to pile pasta on my plate.

Really, I just needed to be close to him.

He glanced up, his smile faltering as he saw whatever it was he saw on my face. "You okay?"

I tried to brighten my expression. "Tired from all that running around."

"Okay." He studied me another moment, then nodded down at my empty plate. "Here for some stellar carbs?"

"Load me up."

While everyone filled their plates, my unease settled a little. I was probably blowing things out of proportion. They were just poking fun at my lack of athletics. That was what friends did, right? No big deal.

But as the conversations continued on—about shows I hadn't watched and music I didn't care about—I felt left out. Like every time we got together. Which was stupid. Logan and I had plenty of things in common. I could talk about any of them with him.

Yet he was talking with his friends. I couldn't interrupt that. So I sat quietly and listened to the banter and the discussions, the yelps of "I can't believe they did that!" and "Remember that concert in Philly?" I ate my pasta, soaked in the warmth and the sunshine, and rested against Logan's shoulder, trying to ignore those feelings. This was his family, and they were important to him. I wouldn't fuck this up by being a sourpuss.

I was jostled from my self-reflection by a phone alarm going off, followed by a series of groans. I glanced around, a little confused.

"Jacob has a date," Logan said, making it clear I'd missed something. "And since Troy's drugs are wearing off, I think we're going to head home."

"Okay. Sorry. All that running around and good food must have put me into a trance." I smiled sleepily at him, and he leaned over and kissed me.

"I hope you're not too tired for a bike ride."

A *zing* of excitement shot through me, and I perked up. "No way."

He grinned and nosed my cheek. "Then come on, let's help pack up."

With everyone involved, it didn't take long, and soon we were walking back to where the vehicles were parked. Getting up and focusing on the tasks had woken me up—or perhaps *distracted me* was a better word choice—keeping my thoughts off of everyone's approval. Plus I'd had excitement thrumming through me: I was going to be riding on a motorcycle. Even if it was called *bitch seat*, as Logan had amusedly told me.

As we left, though, some of those doubts returned. I kept playing over their teasing and laughter. Their frustrations during the game: the snappy comments and terse commands. I really hadn't fit in.

Logan slipped his arm around my waist as we walked, and pulled me close. "What's up?"

I blinked and glanced over to him. His eyes were still crinkled in the corners, his face flushed from a day in the sun and outdoors. "Huh? Um, nothing. Tired I guess."

The smile faltered, flickering away. When it returned, it was sadder than before. "Is that it?"

He'd had a fantastic day with his friends, and I wasn't going to be the one to cast a gray pallor. Better to keep my mouth shut. I wrestled up a smile of my own. "Yeah." I turned my smile a little lurid. "But I'm sure a ride on your bike will wake me up."

His deep, rumbling chuckle shuddered through me like a caress down my back. "I'm just glad you had a good day. I know you're more of an indoor cat."

I cranked my head to stare at him. "Wait, what?"

Color darkened his cheeks. "I, uh, sometimes sort of think of you and your friends as indoor cats and my friends as outdoor cats?"

"Okay, aside from the obvious 'Why do you think of our friends as cats?' does this mean that you're an indoor-outdoor cat?"

"Oh definitely. I'm the tom who seduced the indoor cat outside."

I rolled my eyes. "I feel like I should be offended."

"It's not like I really think we're cats."

I snorted. "Yeah, sooo not the point."

We reached his bike, so he tugged me around into a proper embrace, nuzzled against my neck, and trailed his lips up to my ear. "You don't like being the one who was able to tame the wild tom?"

My shiver was entirely a reaction to the whisper of his breath on my skin and not at all related to the thought of taming him. At all. I slid my arms around his neck and nipped his earlobe. "From the wilds of graphic design?"

"Hey," he murmured, all sexy-like, "I'm freelance."

I shook with ridiculous laughter, breaking the spell. His arms tightened around me, and I muffled my amusement against his shoulder, although that made me shake harder.

"It wasn't that funny," he said.

"I dunno," I managed to snort out. "*Free*lance."

He pulled back a little, though my forehead was still resting on his collarbone. "Maybe I should leave you behind. No ride on my bike."

I gasped and stared up at him, widening my eyes in the exact exaggeration of horror his fake threat warranted. "No! Please! What can I do to get your forgiveness?"

He kissed me—barely a brush of our lips. "I think forgiveness is better earned at home." Another kiss, which I tried to chase but was denied. "Your place?"

I sighed, reluctantly moving out of his arms. "Okay."

He unlocked his helmet from the bike and handed it over. We'd already made sure it fit me, and he'd be wearing the secondary one that fit in his saddlebags. The helmet still felt huge on my head, and I probably looked like one of those Funko Pop! figurines. He, of course, fit the part with his black leather jacket, sleek helmet, and boots. I wanted to jump him, wrap my legs around his waist, and go at it.

Instead I paid attention to the probably important specifics of where I should sit and place my feet and hands.

"You can grip the seat here." He pointed to a spot below the seat.

"Or I can put my arms around you."

He smirked. "That's the other option."

Getting on was an adventure of *Wait, do I . . .* and *No, put your hand here* and *No, let me . . .* but we eventually were both straddling the bike. I slid forward until my crotch was securely against his ass and my arms around his waist. He patted my thigh and I squeezed them around him.

"Comfortable?"

"Perfect fit." I wished I could whisper it in his ear, but the helmet didn't allow for it.

"Feet up."

I took the position and the bike roared to life. The hum of it spread through me, burrowing into my muscles and sinking into my bones. It was like nothing I'd ever felt before. There was the raw power, yes, but it was also . . . open. No cage to protect me from the world and the road. Yet I didn't feel unsafe. I leaned forward slightly, letting my body press against Logan's. I melted into him, as if the three of us—Logan, the bike, and me—were one being.

And then we began to move.

Even wearing multiple layers, plus the helmet, I swore I could feel the wind. But not just the wind. *Everything.* I could reach out and touch it all. Well, if I could move without tipping us over and ruining the moment.

Instead I kept my hands firmly on Logan, our bodies pressed as close together as was possible with clothes on. We were positioned to fuck too, and I wanted to kiss the curve of his spine and shed our clothes and do that. I imagined the bike parked in a private garage, where we could strip off our clothing and fuck over the bike. Obviously I'd have to wait—as it was cold and Logan didn't have a private garage—but that didn't mean my hands couldn't wander, down over his hips and along the insides of his thighs where he straddled the seat.

I didn't get too handsy—not wanting to crash, after all, and wanting to enjoy the ride itself. The vibrations, the world rushing past with nothing between me and it except the helmet, the slight fear when we made a turn and it was like we were going to fall over, the thrill when Logan took the long way home so we could speed down the road without having to worry about traffic. We still weren't going too fast, but my heart was racing and the pulse throbbed in my dick.

The downside of taking the long way home was, well, it was a long way home. I enjoyed every torturous minute, but when he finally parked the bike by my place, I was beyond ready to get off.

I marched up the stairs with Logan's hand in mine, a bag of stuff over each of our shoulders, and a hard-on in my pants that made marching less than ideal.

Once we'd gotten to my apartment, we had to go to the kitchen to throw some items into the fridge. I thought I was going to weep with joy when I slid the last cold item onto the shelf and let the door swing closed. Finally. I turned, my eyes set on Logan. He was reaching for his bag again, but I slipped in front of him, our chests together and our eyes locked.

"It can wait."

He stretched his arms around me and pinned his hands to the counter, lodging me firmly between his hips and the immoveable. His cock pressed against me, and I inhaled sharply. Grinning, he lowered his forehead to mine. "Can it?"

"The food can," I growled, tilting my chin up to meet his lips in a consuming kiss. He tasted of the cake he'd eaten and the coffee he'd washed it down with, so I delved deeper, until all I could taste was him. Until he overwhelmed my senses and I was only aware of his hand moving to grip my lower back, his tongue teasing mine in their dance. I thrust forward, and he groaned, sending a shiver down my spine. God, I wanted him.

I wanted him always. I wanted to drag myself home from work and find him here. I wanted to leave together when we went on trips like today's. I wanted to experience all the little moments that connected his life. And I wanted him to experience mine.

The throb in my groin warred with the thump of my heart, but I pulled back slightly, panting against his lips. He rocked his hips, as if to remind me of what we were doing, but didn't plunge ahead.

Instead, he waited while I scrabbled at the words that were a jumble in my head.

"You know, we could have fucked this morning if we lived together." Eloquent I was not.

Thankfully he understood me. "Are you saying that you want to move in together?"

An exciting, terrifying tremor slammed through me. "Yes. If you want to. I mean, of course if you want to. You wouldn't agree if you didn't want to—"

He shut me up with a kiss, thankfully. His next words were chuckled against my lips. "So you want to move in because it's *convenient*."

He was laughing at me, but I could hear the yes in those words. "I wanted to point out the various benefits." I ground my hips forward once, slowly. "But if you don't want to."

"Oh, I do—" He was cut off by the shrill scream of my phone, the other hard thing in my pants. He sighed, undoubtedly recognizing the ringtone I'd set for my mother. "You have to take that, don't you?"

I groaned, contemplating, for a moment between rings, not answering. But then the screech sounded again and I remembered that she would keep calling until she reached me. She said that since she didn't call often, I should always be available to talk to her. I shoved my hand between Logan and me and whipped out my phone. He didn't back off a millimeter.

I put the phone to my ear and rested my forehead against his shoulder. "Hello."

"Hi, dear! I hope I'm not interrupting!" She always said that, but never actually asked if she was. "I wanted to confirm that you'll be down for your father's birthday."

This was the first I was hearing about it. "Um, are we doing something special?" Usually I sent a card. Although at least now I'd been reminded that I needed to buy a card.

"Yes. I told you"—she most certainly had not—"because he's turning fifty this year, we wanted to have a special to-do. And it falls on Father's Day, so it's pretty much meant to be! You did keep the nineteenth open, didn't you?"

I quickly put her on speaker so I could check the calendar in my phone, and Logan finally stepped back with a muffled sigh. I had a movie marathon scheduled with my friends for the eighteenth, but I'd be fine for the nineteenth. "Yep. I wouldn't forget about this event that you hadn't told me about."

"Don't you take that tone with me, young man. I most certainly told you about this." She sniffed. "But good. I'll see you then. I'll take care of all the food, but be sure to get your father a gift. And will you be bringing anyone special?"

Logan's head shot up, his dark eyes meeting mine, and I switched the phone off speaker and pressed it to my ear, my own gaze dropping to Logan's feet. "Uh, no."

Logan took a step back.

"You really should work on having someone in your life, honey. I hate to see you alone."

I locked my eyes with Logan's. "I'm not alone."

His stony expression softened.

"Then you should bring her!"

I winced. "There's no 'her,' Mom."

And his expression clouded over again. *Damn it.*

"Then you are alone. I know your friends mean a lot, but it's not the same as having someone special, who you love, who shares all of life's struggles and successes with you! By your age I already had your father and you. You don't want to die alone, do you?"

I was so startled, and distracted by Logan's downcast face, that I blurted, "Jesus, Mom, that's morbid!"

She sniffed. "It's the facts of life. I just want you to be happy. And give me grandkids."

I sighed as Logan turned away and began emptying the bags we'd brought up. "Okay, Mom. I'll see you on the nineteenth. I've gotta go."

"Okay, dear. Don't forget a present!"

"Yeah. Love you, bye."

"Byeee!"

I hung up and shoved my phone into my pocket. "Sorry about that."

"Yeah?" He slid a box onto a cupboard shelf and then turned back to face me. "Which part are you sorry for? The interruption? Not telling your mom about me? Not taking me to another family event?"

"It's not that easy," I said, to avoid having to analyze which I *was* sorry for.

"I know!" He slammed his hand down on the counter edge and gripped it hard, as if it was holding him up. "I know, Isaac. But it's been six months. What happened to 'I'll tell them when it's serious'?"

I didn't have an answer for him, but the thought of telling them, of losing them, made my insides quake with fear.

"Or is this not that serious?" Logan asked, voice cracking.

"You know it is! I want to move in with you. Isn't that something?"

He stared at me for a long, long moment. He looked hurt, and angry, and . . . decided. It was the last that made my stomach lurch and curl in on itself. I was terrified of what decision he'd reached.

I wet my lips with a dry tongue and croaked, "I love you."

Maybe he didn't hear it. Maybe he was mad enough that he couldn't say the words back. His tone was flat when he finally spoke. "So you want us to live together, but won't tell them about me."

It wasn't a question. "It's not like that."

But it was like that. Exactly like that. And yet the hurt and anger on his face still wasn't a stronger driving force than the terror I felt at the sheer *thought* of telling my parents.

"I see how it is," he said, his words building into a growl as he continued. "If it's not serious enough for you to tell them, then I don't think we should move in together."

"But—"

"No! I won't be your 'roommate' or your 'good friend' or whatever other goddamn lies you'd tell them to explain why you're living with another man! I—" His head twisted left and right, as if he was searching for something. Unfortunately, he found it. "I have to go."

He snatched his keys from the kitchen table and started toward the front door.

"Wait!"

He didn't wait. Why would he wait for a cowardly piece of trash like me? I ran to the door after him.

"I'll tell them!"

He froze—as still and icy as my insides. But they didn't thaw like his expression when he slowly turned to face me. "You will?"

"But . . . but not yet."

Any hope that had begun to take shape on his face cracked and flaked away.

"Logan, I'm not ready."

"I know." He inhaled deeply. Twice. "But I also don't think you're ready to move in together." He spun back around. "I should go."

I grabbed his arm, all my words clogged in my throat, trying to get out but unable. My desperation must have made its way through my touch, because he folded his hand over mine—warm and comforting in its tenderness.

"Not for good. This isn't goodbye. I just need to leave."

He pried my hand off, kissed my knuckles, then let go. My arm fell like a deadweight beside me. I could only stare as he shoved his feet back into his boots and walked out the front door. It closed with a *thud* that felt more permanent than his words had promised.

He'd said it wasn't goodbye, but he was still gone.

CHAPTER TEN

That night, as I lay alone in my bed, my thoughts wouldn't shut up. Mostly a stream of *He's gone, he's gone, he's gone*, but also echoes of everything he'd said reverberating through my skull and shivering down my bones. It all felt unfair. I shouldn't have to come out to my parents if I wasn't ready. But then he shouldn't have to move in with someone who couldn't be completely honest about their relationship.

I wanted him here. I wanted to not think about telling my parents and what that would mean. I wanted him beside me, his warm body a source of strength and comfort instead of the soft, cold pillow I was wrapped around in his stead. To get him back—even if he hadn't technically *left*—I just had to do one simple, huge thing.

He wasn't asking too much, I supposed. It wasn't like this was some teenage drama and I'd be kicked out of my house and have to live destitute on the streets. The only thing I'd risk losing was my family. And not all of my family. But most of it. My parents.

The thought hardened the knot in my stomach.

I'd lose my parents, but I'd keep Sue. I'd prove to Logan that I loved him. That I wasn't ashamed. Not that I thought he thought I was ashamed.

Maybe I thought I was ashamed. Maybe I was ashamed. Not of him. He was amazing. But of myself. Knowing how my parents would react made a wave of shame wash through me: I wasn't being a good son, I was a disappointment, I was ruining the family.

Yet if I let that shame and guilt win, I would never be happy, because I'd never fully have Logan.

Fuck.

Maybe I wasn't giving my parents enough credit. Maybe they'd be understanding—after a while. I mean, they hadn't loved the idea of Logan when he'd been supposedly dating Sue, but they'd been courteous to him. And I could explain that he was educated and doing well for himself—not that those things made him a better man, but my parents would think so. I'd trade the thug-life image he'd presented with being gay. It all balanced out, right?

Fuck. I didn't know anymore. The thought of telling them had become this monster in my mind—I no longer knew what was real and what was fear.

However, there was someone who could tell me. I texted Sue.

How do you think Mom and Dad would react if I came out?

It was late, but my phone rang a second later.

"You're going to tell them?" Sue said as soon as I'd answered.

"I— Logan— I— Fuck," I finished eloquently. I struggled to inhale. "Logan's hurt that I'm hiding him from them and wants me to tell them. And I'm not sure if they'll actually react badly or I just think they will and he has a point, or if . . . I dunno." I sighed. "Tell me."

Her exhalation was a staticky murmur across the line. "I can't tell you whether you should tell them or not. And Logan shouldn't be forcing you to either. I mean, Zacky, they wouldn't take it well. I don't know if they'd outright disown you, but they'd ignore it or try to talk you out of it. Mom would definitely ignore it, I think." Her voice softened, until I could barely hear it. "I don't think Dad would take it well."

My stomach sank. I had wanted her to tell me that it was all in my head. That it would all be okay. I swallowed. "Thanks."

"I'm sorry. I wish I could— I wish they wouldn't. But you'll always have me. I love you."

My voice cracked twice before I managed to say, "I love you too."

A moment of silence hung between us, and then she said, "So Logan's pushing for you to tell them?"

"Yeah. Mom called about Dad's birthday, and Logan wanted . . . We'd been talking about moving in together."

"That's great!"

I winced. "Yeah. But when I wouldn't tell Mom and Dad about us, he changed his mind. Said if I wouldn't, then he didn't think it was serious enough, didn't think I was serious enough about it to move in together."

The sharp sting of hurt hadn't faded at all over the hours, and it washed fresh across my heart with renewed intensity.

"Well"—I could hear the grimace in her voice—"he shouldn't pressure you, but . . ."

"But you see his point," I finished.

"Yeah. Like what did you think when I told you about my sudden boyfriend that I was bringing to Christmas?"

"That you were ashamed of us." I sighed. "Or him."

"Yeah. I'm sure he doesn't *think* you're actually ashamed of him, but he probably still *feels* that you are. You know?"

I squeezed the pillow I was hugging. "I know."

She gave a long yawn. "So do you know what you're going to do?"

"No. Well." Another swallow to dislodge the lump in my throat. It didn't help. "I'm going to talk to him and try to make it better. As good as I can. As for Mom and Dad? I have no clue."

"I'm sorry. Good luck."

My laugh was hollow. "Thanks."

We hung up, but despite my emotional exhaustion, sleep was a long time in coming.

I woke to a gentle kiss on my temple and the faint smells of exhaust and spring air. Without checking, I knew it was Logan, and a smile crinkled across my face. When I finally opened my eyes, I found him leaning over me, one hand braced on the headboard and the other on the mattress by my shoulder.

He looked like shit. Dark smudges under his eyes, a day's scruff on his face, and a flatness to his skin, like the life had drained out. I felt guilty for lying in bed, for having slept. He didn't seem to have gotten much, if any, rest.

I reached up, cupped his cheeks, and traced my thumbs along the corners of his mouth. "Morning."

"Morning."

I pulled him down until our foreheads touched. "I missed you."

"Fuck, Isaac, I missed you too." He climbed into my bed fully clothed before I could respond, not that I was complaining. Although as he gathered me in his arms, his clothes were a bit chillier than I was under the blankets, and I shivered. It didn't stop me from drawing him closer.

"I love you," I whispered.

"I love you too." God how those four words soothed the gaping wound from yesterday's unanswered declaration. "And I'm sorry. I know it's hard to tell your family."

"I'm sorry that I'm not ready yet. I—I was thinking about it all last night. I want to tell them, but I'm not ready to lose them."

"I know." He tucked my head against his chest, as if he were protecting me from something. Maybe from his words. "I just . . . don't get it. You have shitty parents—no offense—and they treat you like crap, and yet you keep going back for more—"

A choked grunt escaped me from that punch.

"—but you have great friends who are a better kind of family. *Why* do you keep going back to your parents?"

"They're friends, though. They aren't family." I regretted the words as soon as they left my mouth—his family and his friends were the same to him.

He tightened his arms around me. "Family is made up of people who love you, not people connected by blood. Not people who make you feel guilty and shitty. Not people you feel *obligated* to. You should want to see and help your family because they're family and you love them. Because those you love are family and those who love you are family. Your sister is family. Jackson and Emmett are family. Your parents are . . . biological incubators."

"Jesus," I exhaled, "tell me what you really think."

His arms tightened again. "I want you to be happy."

"Fuck." I wrapped my arms and legs around him as best I could, like some insufficient octopus. "Logan, I want to tell them. I want to not care."

"But you can't."

I winced at the disappointment in his voice. My own words were timid, like a frightened child's, and I hated that I felt that way. "Not yet."

"I understand." *But it still hurts*, I heard unspoken. His arms didn't loosen their hold though. "But do you understand that I don't want to move in together until you're ready to tell them?"

I had known that was the case and hadn't expected it to change but, fuck, it stung. "I do."

"It's not an ultimatum."

It sure feels like one, I wanted to snap back. I held my tongue. Taking a leap into a life together was hard when you weren't sure if the other person's hand was in yours. Of course, knowing that didn't soften the blow. "I still want to move in."

"So do I." He loosened his hold enough to kiss my temple and meet my gaze. "But not yet. When we're both ready."

Ready. My own word used against me. I wished I was stronger—strong enough to be ready. "Okay." I leaned up and kissed him.

A kiss to promise that I would be ready someday, hopefully someday soon. A kiss to let him know how much his patience—well, what showed of his patience—meant to me. Clearly it was hard for him, but he seemed to understand that it was hard for me too. And if he didn't understand everything, he at least was willing to work with me.

The second kiss was filled with the yearning from the night spent apart with hurt and anger in our hearts. It wasn't like we weren't used to sleeping in separate beds, although that had been happening less and less, but last night was the first time we hadn't resolved a problem before separating.

The third kiss happened seamlessly, as natural as breathing. As natural as his hands stroking along my back. My hands met cotton and denim, and I had to dig to get to the flesh. Against his lips, I murmured, "You're wearing too much."

"I didn't want to assume I'd be welcome," he murmured against my lips.

My heart tripped, and I clenched his T-shirt in my fist. "You are always welcome."

"Shh," he whispered, before he kissed me once more, delving deep with his tongue and thoroughly distracting me from what had led us here. Instead, it became vital to get him naked so our skin could touch from toes to mouth. I grabbed the hem of his shirt and tugged, but it was pinned between him and the mattress and only moved a little.

I grunted and tugged again. "Up."

He chuckled and began nibbling on my jaw. "Maybe I should stay dressed and spread you out, swallow you down until you cry out in pleasure. You know—" he nipped, hard, probably leaving a mark, but I didn't care if it was high enough for my coworkers to see "—make up for having a hissy fit."

I snorted and gave up on his shirt, dropping my hands to his pants, where the zipper and buttons were cooperative. "Then maybe I should strip you and spread you out and swallow you down. You know—" I reached in and pulled out his cock, already hardening in my hand "—to make up for being a coward."

He hissed, although I wasn't sure if it was because of what I'd said or because I'd given him a slow, long stroke. "You're not a coward."

"If I—"

He kissed me hard, knotting his fingers in my hair to hold my head still, so I couldn't free my mouth to try to argue.

"You're not a coward," he repeated when he'd finally finished shutting me up. "You just need time."

I sighed against his mouth, the most I was willing to concede, and dragged my palm up his cock and then circled the head.

"Mmm, seems like we both have things to apologize for," he said.

"Then you'd better get naked."

He chuckled again and rolled us over so he was on top. "Bossy."

Spotting the chance, I abandoned his cock to grab his shirt, and this time nothing stopped me from removing it. His muscles seemed to ripple, amplifying them, as the cool air hit his skin. I beamed up at him. "If this is the result, I'll have to be bossy more often."

"You're next." He snagged the top of my boxers and swooped down, taking them off as he went, leaving me reaching for him.

"Not fair, I had a head start." I pointed at his pants. "Off, now."

Hey, if being bossy worked before, right?

Amazingly, it worked again. Kneeling by my feet, he hooked his thumbs in the waist of his pants, his cock protruding through his zipper, bouncing in the air, and tugged them down a few inches. "There, they're off my hips."

I glared. He wiggled them down a bit farther.

"Fine." I lunged up—and if you've ever tried to lunge from a position lying on your back on a soft mattress, you can imagine how graceful I was—grabbed his sides, and twisted us around so he landed on his back. We bounced, and I moved down his body so that when we finally settled, I was there to slide his cock into my mouth.

"Fuck, yes, good."

I would have laughed, but I was too busy tasting his skin, which was salty and a little tart from a long day—he must not have showered. It made the scent of his arousal all the stronger as I buried my nose in his curls.

"Goddamn it," he growled, but he didn't sound the least bit angry. He laced his fingers through my hair and gripped hard, not stopping or pushing me, but letting me feel the force of his strength all the same.

I hummed my approval as I slid off, leaving a path of glistening skin in my wake. I swirled my tongue over the head, tasting where the saltiness was strongest, and resisted taking myself in hand. I wanted to focus on him. I wanted to hear his little cries when I blew cool air on his wet, hot skin. I wanted to feel the twitches of his muscle as I sucked him back down until he was lodged in my throat, almost choking me. I wanted to be completely aware as my throat convulsed around his cockhead and his fingers in turn convulsed in my hair.

"Fuck. Izzy, you're going to make short work of me if you keep that up."

The pet name, pulled out so rarely, made my cock throb. I backed off to catch my breath, and as soon as my lips were clear, he gripped me under my arms and hauled me up.

By pure luck, I straddled him instead of knocking cocks, and I lowered my hips until his cock touched mine. I slid them together—not quite a bump and grind, but like a slow-dance sway. His hands dragged down my sides until they rested on my hips. Soon he was controlling the rhythm of my thrusts and the intensity of the pressure, which left me to focus on kissing him.

I never tired of tasting his lips. I tugged the flesh between my teeth and teased it to swell before laving it with my tongue and soothing the bites. All the while pleasure built in my balls, higher and higher, yet his easy pace didn't quite push me over. As if he wanted to see how far he could push me before I begged.

I was nearly there, the ache in my balls so fierce it was almost painful, when he gave in and wrapped his hand around us. Our cocks gained traction, and with only one hand holding my hip, I was free to thrust as much as I wanted.

And I wanted badly.

His hand was a little rough on the stretched, sensitive skin of my cock, but that only intensified the barely there lubricant that my drying saliva provided as I thrust. It was all I needed. With a shout, I jerked hard, and come spattered his stomach, oozing between our cocks and his hand.

His strokes sped up, and I eased out of his grasp and lowered my mouth to his nipple, sucking the little bud in as he grunted his pleasure. A wet shot hit my chin, and in some primal way it felt like I'd been marked. I would have gotten hard again if I could have. Instead I followed the trail of come down his stomach, cleaning up our messes as I went.

When I reached his cock, he hauled me back up. "Jesus, you're going to kill me."

I met his dark eyes and grinned. "What a way to go."

"You're such a cliché." He raised his head and licked my chin, likely cleaning the come that I'd left there. "And a mess."

"Well, that's your fault."

"Then I need to take responsibility."

He rolled us over and licked my chin a few more times—which was more ticklish than anything—before giving my groin the same treatment I'd given his, although mine was already much cleaner. After a few perfunctory licks, he kissed his way up to my mouth and settled down beside me. He wasn't small enough to lie on my chest, but he worked as a blanket, and rested his head beside mine on the pillow.

I turned toward him so we were nose to nose and he could see into my eyes. "I'm sorry that I'm not ready. I want to be—I want so hard to not make myself a liar—but it's too scary still."

"Scarier than losing me?" He winced. "No, don't answer that. It's not a question, and it's not an ultimatum. I'm not going to make you choose between me and them."

I twisted so we were chest to chest and I could wrap my arm around his waist. "You'd win."

He sighed, come-scented breath and all. "It doesn't feel that way."

No, it probably didn't. But I felt like a rock lodged in dry, barren earth. Staying was easier, even if I could see the blossoms a foot over. "By the end of the year, I promise."

His smile wobbled, like he wanted it to be there but it was too hard. "Don't do that to yourself."

I tilted up so I could kiss him lightly. "It's not an ultimatum for myself. It's a deadline. Something for me to get comfortable with so when I do it, I'll feel ready." At his raised eyebrow, I added, "Hopefully."

He returned the kiss, letting the words form between us. "I'll try to be patient."

CHAPTER ELEVEN

I swore my parents' house was getting farther away. It didn't help that Logan was sleeping in and I had to make the long drive on my own, through pouring-down rain, without even his voice to serenade me—because no way in hell was I waking him up early just to talk to me on my trip down.

No, my only company was the knowledge that coming out to my parents would solve a lot of my complaints. All of my complaints, actually. Not that I spent the entire drive thinking about it.

Nope, definitely not.

The weather began to cooperate as I got closer to their place, with the rain stopping and the clouds overhead clearing. It was downright sunny when I pulled into their driveway. I parked next to my sister's car, grabbed my father's present, and headed inside.

Same thing, different day. I wasn't inside more than a minute before Mom was harping that I didn't wrap the present right—Sue and I shared a look—she complained that she had to do all the cooking—Sue and I shared another look—and my father grumbled about his computer acting up.

So, being the not-completely-terrible son that I am, I offered to check it out.

"Nah, you're here as a guest. I don't want to waste your time."

"It's no big deal. I'm sure I'll be able to tell if it's an issue you should go into the shop for or if it's something I can fix in a jiffy."

"Don't you think if it was easy that I would have figured it out?" Dad snapped.

"Um, I spend a lot of time around computers, so I thought—"

"It ain't an easy fix!" he shouted.

"Certainly. Sorry." My stomach churned and tension strung my shoulders up tight. "Uh, good luck with it, then."

"Least the Best Buy won't have some damned Oriental helping me," Dad grumbled, and Sue and I winced. "I tried calling that help line, and it was a complete waste of time. Couldn't understand a goddamn word."

I was reminded of why I tried to avoid starting conversations with my dad. "I had a similar problem when I called— Well, I can't remember what it was for, but the person who answered had a Deep South accent. Sweet as could be, but I had to ask a thousand times for her to repeat herself!"

I laughed—only a bit forced—because gosh darn, couldn't thick accents just happen all over?

"She was probably black."

My laugh died. "Since it wasn't a Skype call, I couldn't tell you. So Sue, did you have a nice drive here?"

Maybe we switched conversations on Dad a bit too often, because he didn't even blink at the sudden change.

Sue launched into an overly detailed description of her drive and the traffic and the construction, and I'd never been more enthralled to hear about the potholes that had sprung up around her town over the winter. Finally we were distracted by the arrival of snacks. It was a godsend.

Mom littered the table with chips, dip, crackers, and nuts, then went back to the counter for a second round, because obviously what she'd provided wasn't enough for four people. I shook my head and reached for a paper plate.

"Whoops!"

Something hit my back, and the unmistakable feeling of cold wetness soaked through my shirt. I glanced over my shoulder as Mom peeled off the plate she was holding, which contained a smashed brick of cream cheese that had once been covered in cocktail sauce. The red offered a nice contrast to my sky-blue shirt.

"Oh my gosh! I'm so sorry!" She set aside the plate and began attacking me with paper towels, which got the worst of it off but seemed to be grinding some of it in. "C'mon, if we're quick and throw it in the wash, I bet it won't even stain." She held out her hand.

Grateful to get the wet, sticky thing off, I slunk out of it, trying my best to avoid smearing sauce all over myself. I held up the shirt once I was free and grimaced at the mark. The shirt seemed doomed, but I handed it over, and Mom bustled away to do a bit of laundering.

"What the fuck is on your back?"

Sue gasped, although it probably wasn't because she'd seen the black ink trailing down my spine.

Play it cool, play it cool, play it cool, I told myself as I turned around. Dad's face was red and his lip twitched in its grimace. I tried on the innocent smile I hadn't worn since I was a teen trying to get out of trouble. "My tattoo?"

"Yes, your goddamn tattoo," Dad snarled. "When the hell did that happen!" Not so much a question as an accusation. His eyes flickered down and narrowed. "What the hell are those?"

I dropped my gaze down to my nipple piercings. *Goddamn motherfucking shit.* I cleared my throat. "Yeah, I got these and the tattoo a couple years ago," I said, flooding my voice with confusion. "I thought I told you guys about them."

"You most certainly did not!" He highlighted this fact by standing and slamming his palms against the kitchen table, which creaked under the weight. I forced myself not to flinch. "Why would you mark yourself with something so fucking queer?"

So the whole world will know I'm gay, Dad.

Because I am fucking queer.

There were options for me to take this and run with it. Pull all the Band-Aids off at once, as it were. But as I met my dad's glaring blue eyes, my cowardice once again took front and center. Being shirtless didn't help, and I had to struggle not to cover myself and cower. "Dad, tattoos and piercings aren't 'queer.' Lots of people have them these days."

"Yeah, bikers and rapists. Like that waste-of-space Logan your sister brought home," he growled, taking a step toward me.

"Hey! Don't talk sh— Uh. Be nice about Logan. He's my friend." My heart raced. As if my dad would pick up on the inflection on the word *friend* and realize how much of a friend he was.

"And mine." Sue moved to stand next to me, creating a united front. I wanted to sag against her. Hell, I wanted to hide behind her.

Instead, I leaned slightly so our shoulders brushed, and I took what comfort I could from that.

Outnumbered, Dad shrugged, still huffing. "I don't see why you'd do that to yourself. Paint yourself as one of *those* people."

I wasn't going to ask which group of people I was painting myself as. Maybe just as a person who had tattoos. Who the fuck knew. "I like the way it looks."

That was easier than saying I'd gotten it when my first boyfriend broke up with me. Not as a reminder of him, but that I had a spine and all pain healed over. Plus I did like the art.

Dad snorted. "We'll see how you feel about it when you're sixty and can't find a woman who will take you like that."

"Dad," I said, perfectly calmly, as if this conversation wasn't making my palms sweat, "lots of people with tattoos get together. Maybe the person I'll end up with will have tattoos."

I could almost feel Sue fighting the urge to roll her eyes.

"Well, I don't like it. And you've broken your mother's heart." Dad stepped back and returned to his seat, as if the conversation was done. And maybe it was. He'd said his part; he'd shown me the errors of my ways. Nothing else he could do since he couldn't take me over his knee anymore.

I sighed in relief.

"What was all that yelling about?" Mom asked as she emerged from the basement where the laundry machines were. I didn't get a chance to turn around—as if flashing my piercings instead of the tattoo would be better—before she gasped. "Oh, baby, what did you do to yourself?"

"Actually a tattoo artist did it," I said, because I couldn't seem to control myself. Logan would have laughed and given me a kiss, if only to shut me up.

Sue rolled her eyes so hard the axis of the planet changed.

Mom huffed. "You know what I mean."

"Uh, well, I got a tattoo and piercings. I could have sworn I told you. Do you like them?" I asked, knowing she wouldn't. But she also wouldn't react like Dad, ready to skin my hide, so it was safe to ask and play the fool.

"It's not what I would have done, dear." She sighed the sigh of all put-upon mothers. "But it's your body. As long as you're ready to live with them for the rest of your life."

I never understood why people said that. Did they assume most people got tattoos so that they'd go away? I mean, I understood the thought, *You won't want this when you're older*. But my line of thinking was that there were going to be a lot of things I didn't like when I got older, so I certainly wasn't going to regret a little bit of ink on my skin.

The old saying got it wrong: live fast, die young, and leave a good-looking corpse. Nah, I want my corpse to be well lived in.

Mom probably wouldn't want us talking about death at my dad's birthday though. "I'm hoping it lasts a very long time, personally."

She sniffed. "Well, we should probably cover you up. Wouldn't be proper at the dinner table. Rupert, get him a T-shirt, would you?"

My father shoved a salsa-drenched chip in his mouth and grumbled around it as he stood and left the kitchen.

"Thanks, Dad!"

I heard the grumbling echo down the hall. I tried really hard not to smile. Sue elbowed me in the side.

"Ow!"

"Now, now, that's no way to behave," Mom chided before I could exact my revenge.

I narrowed my eyes at Sue. "You better watch it."

"Oooh, whatcha gonna do?"

I opened my mouth, paused, then closed it, smiling widely. "Nothing at all."

She went from playful to suspicious in an instant, and I fought off a wider smile. Paranoia was a wonderful tool for revenge.

Dad came back down and handed me a . . . well, I'll call it a shirt. It had to be his oldest, rattiest, mow-the-lawn-and-work-in-the-garage shirt. Once white, it was now pale gray, although *translucent* was a better description. Tiny holes lined the hem, and brownish stains hugged the armpits. It was going to be more disgusting to have to stare at this than my bare chest.

Sue leaned over, smug joy on her face, and whispered, "If you'd like, I think I have a spare shirt in my car."

She was at least two sizes smaller than me, but I was really tempted to take her up on the offer. Instead I gritted my teeth and pulled the shirt on. Despite appearances, it felt clean, though it sagged around me like a sad hospital gown.

"Thanks, Dad." I hoped he couldn't hear the grimace in my voice or see the one I was keeping off my face.

"Yeah, just try not to get it dirty."

"Definitely not." I glanced down at the revolting shirt and had the sudden urge to send Logan a selfie. This torture might just make up for everything else I'd done.

I did end up sneaking into the bathroom and sending Logan a picture. He was all sympathy, although I could practically hear his attempts to hold back his laughter. He kept me sane as the day went, forwarding GIFs and videos, telling me of his own minor frustrations with a personal project he was working on, possibly blowing them out of proportion to make me smile.

My mom noticed my focus on the phone, of course, and immediately began harping on me about it and warming up for the "sins of ignoring your family in favor of your phone" speech. I wasn't sure if Sue was saving me when she told Mom, "Obviously he's in love."

"You have a girlfriend!" Mom screeched, which made Dad complain and turn up the volume on an infomercial. Why did I get in trouble for checking my phone when he was in the room next to us not participating in our conversation at all? I'd have said it was because it was his birthday (and he could ignore us if he wanted), but it was par for the course.

"Um," I said in reply to Mom. "I'm seeing someone. Yeah."

"Why didn't you bring her?" It sounded more like an accusation than a question. I probably deserved having to deal with this questioning at home and here.

"We weren't ready yet, Mom. You know how intense it is to meet the family."

Mom sniffed. "You and Sue make it sound like bringing someone here is like running the gauntlet."

"That's because it is. You didn't even like Logan and you asked if he wanted children and how many!"

"I want little grandbabies. You guys aren't getting any younger."

"It is a certainty of time," I muttered.

"What?"

"Nothing." I sighed. "Mom, *if* we get happily wedded off, it's still not guaranteed that you're going to have grandchildren anytime soon. If at all."

She gaped at me as if I'd ritualistically slaughtered a puppy in front of her and was now eating the entrails. If the puppy was her hopes and dreams, it was sort of true. Sue didn't disagree with me, but she didn't come to my rescue either. I couldn't blame her. I already regretted telling Mom the hard truths.

"Why wouldn't you give me grandchildren?"

Roe and their English degree could probably dissect that sentence into an entire thesis, although it likely would require help from Jenna's psychology and sociology research. I had the benefit of none of these and, honestly, I didn't want to think too hard about the fact that Mom only wanted us to have kids in order for her to have grandchildren, not for us to experience the delights of child-rearing.

"Some people aren't meant to be parents," I told her.

"You can always adopt."

As if pure physical capabilities were what would stop us. "I'm sure we'll keep it in mind. I'm just saying that you shouldn't hang all your hopes on grandkids, okay?"

She didn't appear very happy with this pronouncement, but she let it go—although she favored Sue in all conversation after that. Which, really, wasn't the worst thing that could have happened. I escaped into the living room with Dad, and we watched a rerun of a football game from 1978. I kid you the fuck not. But at least he didn't care that I spent the whole time texting, as long as my notifications were on silent.

Eventually we had cake and ice cream and gave him his presents. Then I got my shirt back and Sue and I escaped.

By some magic, I got home in record time. And by *home*, I meant Logan's place, since that was where he was, hunched over his drawing tablet, headphones on. Thankfully he heard me knock on the door of his office, because sneaking up on him would probably result in being stabbed with the stylus.

Instead he threw down his electronics and swooped me up in a hug.

He lifted me easily with his bulging muscles, and I laughed as he spun me around once. I hooked my arms around his neck and met his lips for a kiss, grateful for the warmth and familiarity there. God, how wonderful would it be to be greeted like this every time I came home?

Or, my mind not-so-helpfully supplied, *he could have joined you for the entire day and you wouldn't need to crumble into his support now.*

I pushed aside the thought. Not ready. Not yet. Right now I simply wanted to enjoy the strength he was wrapping me in.

We were both a little breathless with kisses and laughter when he set me down again.

"Welcome home," he murmured against my lips.

I kissed those perfect lips. "Glad to be home. Did you have a good day?"

"I went for a ride, worked, got frustrated, went to the gym, worked, got frustrated, went for a ride."

"Texted me constantly to keep me from committing, um, patricide but both parents."

"Parricide."

I quirked my brow. "I'm not going to ask."

"It was on *Jeopardy*."

"What, today?" When he shook his head, I gaped. "Your memory is impressive."

"I had a vision that I would need the word sometime in the future."

"Ha-ha."

He kissed my nose, then pulled back so he could wrap an arm around my shoulders and lead us out of the office and into the living room. "It sounded like you had a shit day."

I sighed. "It could have been worse. They actually handled my tattoo and piercings pretty well. My dad was only completely disgusted, not horribly disgusted, and Mom just felt like I'd mutilated my body and no one would ever love me."

Logan growled, manhandled me to the couch, and seated me sideways so he could sit behind me. At first I wasn't sure why, since this wasn't comfortable for the snuggling—and sex—I wanted, especially since he'd left a good amount of distance between us. Then he leaned over and kissed the faint brownish-red stain on the back of my shirt. "We need to get you a new shirt."

"Uh, sure?"

He nipped at my neck—at least, I thought that was what he was doing. Then I felt him take the neck of my shirt in two fists. In movies, you always see the guy rip his shirt off to reveal his rippling, bulging muscles. I'd read somewhere that ripping shirts like that is actually really hard, so I expected Logan to try and then us to have a laugh, and I'd take my shirt off like a normal person.

Riiiiiiip.

There was a reason ripping off shirts was so popular in fiction. It was fucking hot—even if it choked me a little when he first pulled. Suddenly the cool air was brushing my skin, the tattered edges of the shirt tickling me as he reached the bottom and dropped the two flaps.

Holy fuck. I wanted to turn around, straddle his waist, and ride his dick. Like now. Immediately.

Before I could begin to put my plan into action though, his lips touched the top of my back, on my spine, where my circuit-board tree tattoo began.

"This is beautiful." His warm breath whispered against my skin, and I broke out in goose bumps. "It's not fucking *mutilation*."

I shivered and closed my eyes, a smile tugging at the corners of my lips. "You might be biased, Mr. Full-sleeves."

He traced a line of the circuit board with his tongue, then kissed the tip of the "leaves." His words blew gently on the wet skin. "I'd rather be biased than bigoted."

Without waiting for a reply, he continued tracing the lines that made up my tattoo, wiping away the hate it had been plastered with today and painting it in his kisses instead. It was so fucking cliché, and yet I could feel the weight that had dragged down my shoulders all day slowly falling away with each caress.

When he kissed the last root circuit, I exhaled deeply. The stress was gone. "You're magic."

He kissed my shoulder, my neck, then gripped my chin to draw my lips close enough to meet his. I was pulled backward, so my skin was against the cotton of his shirt, and he wrapped his other arm around me, holding me still as he claimed my mouth. I felt defenseless and laid bare, and I wasn't afraid in the least.

I was free.

The hand on my chin stroked down my neck to my chest, pinning me to him. His forefinger teased over my nipple, trailing back and forth and catching on the stud as he deepened the kiss. I moaned, pushing off the couch, arching up into the contact.

The finger strumming my nipple stopped, and the hand slid down, hooked around my side, holding me secure. I didn't want to seem needy, but his strength was so easy to fall into, to be comforted by. Plus it never made me feel weak. My whole body sighed contently, knowing *here* I was strong in relying on his strength.

When my muscles relaxed, my whole body softening in his embrace, he finally broke the kiss. "There you go."

"Magic," I repeated.

He hummed and shifted us slightly so we could both lie comfortably on the couch. His words were more solemn, though, when he spoke. "I know they're your family, but you hate visiting them. They're horrible to you. I don't get why you're so afraid of losing them."

I tensed, but his arms tightened. Not trapping me, but holding me close. Like it was a promise that he wasn't starting a fight but was telling me what he was thinking. He didn't want to argue; he wanted to understand.

"They're my parents. My family."

It was probably a weak excuse, but it was the only thing I had.

"So? They don't treat you like family should."

I sighed. I didn't want to argue about this, not right now. I didn't even want to talk about it. "But they're the one I've got."

He opened his mouth, but must have seen something in my expression, because he closed it and kissed me instead. "Welcome home."

A smile broke the tension that had started to form. It didn't matter that we weren't sharing a place, that this wasn't *my* home.

Because I was in his arms, and that was enough. "Nowhere else I'd rather be."

CHAPTER TWELVE

"I can't believe you abandoned your boyfriend at a party in order to come hang out with us."

I looked up from the little skull cookies I was arranging on a platter. Jackson was retaping some orange streamer that had fallen, although I wasn't sure why. Why he was fixing it, that was; I was pretty sure gravity was the reason it had fallen, since Rosa definitely couldn't get up that high. "You mean why I'd want to come to a party that everyone else bailed on, where I'm going to be hanging out with my two friends and their daughter and handing out candy, instead of going with my super-hot boyfriend to an adult party where I could be getting drunk and making out with said super-hot boyfriend?"

"Well, when you put it that way . . . Yes, why the hell are you here?"

I set the cookies on the table with the other food that was meant to feed six and would be feeding three. I saw leftovers in my future. "Part of it is because I said I'd come here first and I felt bad that everyone else bailed on you. Also, Emmett promised me his special deviled eggs. But! The real reason is that Logan's friends have been having drama again. I got the impression he was going to their party to keep the peace and would rather be here with me. He *insisted* I come here. I think he's going to use me as an excuse to bail if things get bad."

Emmett must have heard me, because he laughed as he came down the stairs with Rosa in his arms. "So he's using you to bail on a fun party and come to a party that everyone else bailed on because it wasn't fun?"

I frowned. "This party is going to be rockin'—by which I mean, rockin' the baby to sleep, but . . ." I snapped a cookie in half. "I can't believe everyone else 'had another party to go to.'"

"Yeah," Jackson said. "I thought at first you guys were all getting together without us—because hanging with a baby is so not cool—but then you were still free, so I guess I was wrong."

My frown deepened. What if everyone *was* having a party, but they hadn't wanted to invite me either? I shook my head, trying to clear that thought. "We'll have to send them pictures from all the fun we're having and make them jealous."

"Well, least the decorations look good," Jackson said, climbing down from his stepladder. "Oh, and the food smells great! Although are you going to eat that demolished cookie or continue poking its eyehole?"

I stared at the cookie I had broken into quarters, then popped one of the pieces into my mouth. "Eat."

Jackson rolled his eyes and took Rosa from Emmett, who then went to pull the last few items from the fridge, including the promised deviled eggs made with sriracha, which I immediately swiped from his hands so I could help myself to one.

"Your addiction to those eggs is a little terrifying," Jackson said.

"You're just worried my love of them is going to make me want to woo Emmett away from you, and then you won't have any eggs for yourself."

Emmett snorted. "So both of you only love me for my eggs?"

I snorted in reply. "Obviously."

"No," Jackson said, going over to kiss Emmett's cheek. "I also keep you around to do the dishes."

They pretended to bicker back and forth, so I stole another egg and went around the house to turn off all the house lights (and to turn the porch light on). The living room was cast in an orange glow from the strings of lights framing the windows and the seemingly thousands of candles—most of them battery powered—scattered around the space.

"Nice mood lighting," I called to them.

"I figured it'd be good for telling"—Emmett did something weird with his voice, dropping it and making it waver—"spoo-ooky stories."

"And have Jackson sleep-deprived from being unable to sleep for a week?"

Jackson came in, Rosa in his arm, a plate in the opposite hand. "I think he meant baby-appropriate spooky stories. Unless he wants to sleep on the couch."

"Did you just call yourself a baby?"

Jackson gave me an unimpressed look, and I smiled, all earnest good boy, but it must have been lost in the dim lighting. He shook his head. "Emmett, can you bring my beer in?"

He set his plate down on the coffee table, then Rosa on the floor, before joining her, pushing the plate as far from her grasp as possible.

I stopped by the kitchen and loaded up my own plate, then joined everyone in the living room. Despite there being plenty of seats, we all were on the floor so we could play with Rosa as she teeteringly walked around. It was strange to think that a year and a half ago she'd been a wrinkly bean that hadn't been good for much more than screaming, eating, and pooping. Now she tried to steal the food off our plates, despite not being quite up to eating most of the things. Cooked vegetables? Yes. Raw whole veggies with ranch? No.

She definitely kept us on our toes.

"So how is Logan?" Jackson asked. "I feel like we haven't seen him in ages."

I smiled, thinking about the last few months. After the fight about coming out to my parents, things had been good. We still hadn't moved in together, but more and more of my stuff was at his place—and his at mine—so that I'd go days without seeing my own apartment. He still visibly struggled every time my mom called, but he hadn't pushed me to come out again, and I hadn't pushed to move in together.

But I was feeling a lot closer to being able to do both.

Jackson cleared his throat. "So, how's Logan?"

Heat flashed across my cheeks all the way to my ears. I must have zoned out. "He's good." I took a sip of hard cider, then stared down the neck. "It's serious."

"We got that," Jackson said, and I could have sworn there was *pride* in his voice. "And I'm glad."

"Yeah. I want to move in together, but . . . he won't until I come out to my parents."

Emmett grunted, and I looked up. He and Jackson were doing some silent communicating, the married equivalent of eye-fucking. Emmett grimaced, Jackson's lips twitched, and then they turned their eyes to me and I wondered if I should apologize for eavesdropping, although I had no idea what had been said.

"That's a little . . ." Jackson paused, as if considering the words carefully, "manipulative. He's trying to force you to—"

"No. No, it's not like, 'I'll dump you if you don't come out.' He's afraid I'm not serious about us. Like, I know he knows I am, but he feels like he's being hidden away and cut out from part of my life. And if my parents were actually a threat—like financially or physically—I don't think he'd consider it."

"Still feels underhanded." Emmett grunted.

"Yeah. But I—I said when we first met that I'd come out to my parents when I met someone who was worth it. So I think he feels that because I'm not coming out, then that means he's not worth it."

"Oh, Zack." Jackson clambered across the floor—and toys—to wrap me in a hug.

It felt unnecessary, but I rested my head on his shoulder anyway while he gave me a firm squeeze.

"I understand how he feels," Emmett said while the hug went on, "but you shouldn't feel obligated to do it for him. Do it when you're ready. If you do it for him, you might end up blaming him for anything that goes down." Emmett slapped his fist into the opposite palm playfully. "Need me to let him know that?"

"Are you threatening to beat up my boyfriend?"

Jackson whispered in my ear, "That's a fight I'd pay to see."

Yeah, thinking about it, it would be hot. Except for the part where one of my best friends and my boyfriend would be beating the shit out of each other.

"Only an emotional bashing," Emmett said, smirking.

I gently broke the hug and sort of pushed Jackson toward Emmett. "Go restrain your husband."

Jackson shrugged and instead went to grab Rosa before she got to his drink. "There's no stopping him. Sorry."

Thankfully we moved on to other topics after that. They seemed to get that I wouldn't cave because of Logan's pressure, although part of me wondered: what was stopping me from telling Mom and Dad? I knew, logically, what I *said* was stopping me, and it *was* stopping me. But I'd told him that if someone meant enough to me, I'd tell my parents.

Logan meant enough. More than enough. Yet here I was, resisting at every turn. So was he right? Was I not committed and that was the real reason I didn't want to? Or had I underestimated my desire to not change the status quo, to not rock the boat, to not face the change that seemed almost inevitable? If that was the case—and I was becoming increasingly terrified and sure that it was—then what was I willing to lose in order for things to remain the same?

A knock at the door snapped me from my fretting, and since Emmett was changing a diaper and Jackson had disappeared into the kitchen, I grabbed the candy bowl and opened the door.

In black leather chaps that hugged his thighs and framed the bulge of his crotch, a leather jacket, and with a helmet tucked jauntily against his hip, the man on the stoop was a little old to be going around begging for candy.

"Trick or treat," Logan said, a dangerous grin curling the corners of his lips.

I held the candy bowl behind my back. "Yeah? And what kind of trick are you going to pull if I don't give you candy?"

He stepped forward, plastering his body against my front as his arms wrapped around me. His lips brushed mine with every word and sharp inhale. "I didn't say it was candy I was after."

He covered my mouth in a kiss as his hands rooted through the candy bowl. It was difficult to fight him when his tongue was making delicious promises in my mouth. His hard body, a solid wall denying any escape, was hot—a sharp contrast to the cool October air that backed him.

"Close the door—you're letting the heat out!" Jackson ordered.

"And giving all the families a show," Emmett added.

Logan grabbed something from the bowl and secured his arm around my waist, doing a fancy dance step to spin us inside and close the door. "Happy?"

"Thank you. Hi, Logan."

"Hi, Jackson." Logan chuckled and kissed my nose. "Hi, Isaac."

"Happy Halloween." I kissed the slight scruff on his chin. "So what sweet treat did you get?"

He held up the candy, and we burst out laughing at the familiar yellow scrawled with the red saying *Sugar Daddy*. "Looks like I picked up the right treat."

"You're terrible." I kissed his jaw again, just to feel the rough stubble against my lips. "You're also here a lot earlier than I was expecting."

Logan grumbled and released me so he could set his helmet on the back of the couch against the wall. "It was becoming a drama-fest."

"Like Christmas?"

"Yes. I'm not sure what the fu—um." He gritted his teeth and waved at Rosa. "I don't know what they're even fighting about. Matti and Alessa are angry with Troy, who is blaming Bryan. Of course, none of them want to talk about it. Erika keeps trying to play mediator, which I think they need, but Troy, and I guess Bryan, keep saying it's unfair because she's dating Alessa and will automatically side with her. Which is kind of a valid point. Jacob is trying to stay uninvolved, and anytime I try to get a clear picture of what's going on, it breaks down into a screaming match."

"And thus you're here."

"Yeah. I told them they needed to talk it out. I suggested Erika lock them in a room with a bottle of rum until they got through it."

"I thought they'd worked it out before New Year's." They had all seemed fine at the party.

Logan glared at the air. "So did I."

"Aw, my poor baby. I'm sorry." I stepped in front of him and snagged the zipper of his jacket, then dragged it down slowly. "But now you're here and we can have fun."

"There are children present," Jackson reminded me.

I cranked my neck around to glare at him. "What do you think I meant? Dirty mind!" I turned back to Logan. "Sit down, relax, and I'll make a plate for you if you'd like."

"Oooh, the service here's nice."

I opened my mouth to make a sugar-daddy joke but was saved from embarrassment by the doorbell ringing. Since I was still holding the candy bowl, I turned to the door as Logan headed for the kitchen. A set of twins dressed as an angel and demon were there.

"Trick or treat!"

"Oh my. What great costumes." I doled out the candy—giving them extra for being creative and adorable—and waved as they left. Then I passed the bowl to Jackson, who was lounging on the couch, sipping his drink.

Jackson winked at me. I rolled my eyes and followed Logan to the kitchen, where he was loading his plate. His playful façade had dropped, and now I could see the tension around his eyes and mouth. After fetching a cider for him from the fridge, I stood close to him as he wavered between the two types of deviled eggs. I bumped his shoulder. "What's up?"

"Trying to pick an egg," he said, not looking up.

I leaned closer, so my words were a soft murmur in his ear. "Why not have both?"

His chuckle was low and exhausted. "Why do I feel like we're not talking about eggs?"

Angling over, I plucked a sriracha egg from the platter and set it on his plate. "What else would we be talking about, hmm?"

I was glad that after ten months together he understood my incompetent attempt to get him to talk about his emotions. I was also glad that he wasn't as incompetent as me.

With the plate in one hand, he took my free hand and led me to a seat. He was smiling, sort of, but tension had his shoulders pulled taut. He sat down, then set his plate on the table and pulled me onto his lap. I came along willingly and put the drink down, so I was free to wrap my arms around his neck and rest my forehead against his.

"What's bothering you?"

"Oh, is that what that meant?"

I nodded, though it was kind of weird with our heads like they were.

He sighed and readjusted me—just picked me up and shifted me on his lap and if this hadn't been a Very Serious Conversation, I would have been turned on by the ease of the manipulation. But this was important, so I sat there, reclined sideways against him with his arm around my back. He moved his plate to my lap and picked at the food as we spoke. "The drama is getting to me, I guess. I hate to see my family fight, you know? They'll work it out, eventually, but for the moment, it's stressful being around them."

I wanted to ask how he knew they'd work it out. There was nothing keeping them all together like blood kept a family together. Like having twenty-plus years together kept a family together. Maybe this argument would become a crack that grew and grew until it shattered their friendship apart. The thought chilled me.

I knew better than to actually *say* that though. Instead I tried to think about conflicts within my own family. Or at least with my sister, since in all other conflicts the victory automatically went to our parents. "Well, sometimes we need to avoid our families until tempers cool down, right? Like, you can't always force things to work out. Sometimes time needs to work its magic."

"So we shouldn't get together at all, then?"

"Maybe don't invite the people who are causing the conflict?"

"That's, like, half the group. And we can't have Erika there without Alessa." He groaned, and I felt useless. There didn't seem to be anything they could do except to tell everyone involved to grow up and get over themselves. Something told me—having met his friends—that they wouldn't take kindly to that.

"I'm sorry," I murmured, tucking myself against his neck. "I wish I could help."

He sighed—not like he was disappointed, but rather like the tension was leaving through his lips. The arm around my waist squeezed. "You being here, having a place for me to go, is help enough."

I kissed his neck, because it was there and how could I not? "I'm here for you always."

"Thank you."

It felt like a promise, like something more than all the *I love you*s we'd said. It was the *always* that did it. That was a forever word. It should have been scary, that promise. The cause of the cold feet that grooms-to-be experienced on their wedding day. But it wasn't. It felt right. I wanted nothing less than forever with him.

No matter what the cost.

My stomach cramped at the thought, because I had a feeling I knew what the cost would be, but I tightened my arm around him and he tightened his around me, and the certainty I felt in my promise was stronger than the fear.

Oh, I thought. *Is this what it means when someone's worth changing everything for?*

"I love you," I whispered. Now wasn't the time to announce that I was willing to rock my world and come out to my parents, but I needed him to know.

He kissed me, and then moved the plate so he could wrap both arms around me without making a mess. "I love you too."

And in those words, I felt all the different sorts of love he had for me. Passionate and romantic, of course, but also the bond of friendship, of being able to rely on each other and support each other.

I was so fucking lucky to have found him.

That sealed the deal. The fear of facing my parents was nothing compared to the fear of not having him here in my life. The decision wasn't about ultimatums; it was about being able to share our lives completely with each other, to always be there to give the other strength.

I clung to this with all the strength I had to give.

The next day we stumbled out of bed exhausted, hungry, and completely satisfied. We'd gone to bed later than we'd planned and had gotten distracted on the coming and the going. Still, there was nothing urgent that we needed to do—only all those boring adult things like cleaning the shower, vacuuming, and maybe dusting. It was getting hard to see through the inch of dust that coated the TV screen.

But first, there was something I needed to do. To tell him. It involved him, after all.

We brewed our coffee, tore into the package of donuts we'd bought, and settled at the table. I fiddled with my phone for a bit, glancing at the various apps I kept up with, but it couldn't hold my attention. So much for a nice relaxing morning breakfast.

"Hey, Logan, can we talk?"

He glanced up from the book he was reading on his tablet, eyebrows quirked. "What is it?"

His gray eyes weren't even that intense, but a flutter of nerves ran through me. I dropped my gaze to my phone, lying on the table, then changed the angle thirty degrees. Then back again. "So, I was thinking about what you said."

A long pause followed, and then he put his hand over mine, which had still been twitching my phone around, and I looked up. He was watching me, a soft smile making him seem open and welcoming. "Oh? Which thing?"

"About coming out. To my parents. Since I'm out to everyone else." I laughed nervously and shook my head. What was wrong with me? This was *Logan*. I shouldn't be anxious. As if I'd needed the reminder, a small bit of tension bled out of my chest. This was Logan, and I loved him. "I want to tell them. I mean, I'm ready to tell them."

His face lit up like a goddamn Christmas tree. "You are?"

It was hard not to match that smile with one of my own. "I am. I'm scared as fuck, but—but you're too important for me to pretend you aren't the best part of every day."

His eyes widened, not so much in surprise but in sappy joy. Warmth flooded through my chest, and I was probably blushing, but I didn't care. I'd done that. I'd made him that happy. And, Jesus, I was doing this for me, but that was a fan-freaking-tastic bonus.

"You're the best part of my days too," he said, eyes still ridiculously wide.

The warmth spreading through me exploded into an intense heat that told me I was definitely blushing. I turned my hand over so I could clasp his, and leaned across the table. He met me halfway.

The kiss was surprisingly soft compared to the tight grip of our hands, but it spoke volumes. It was solid and there. If we hadn't just finished up in the bedroom, I would have dragged us there. Instead, I sat back in my seat, our hands together, and took a sip of coffee. I was still terrified of the thought of telling my parents, and we had a ton of details to work out, but Logan was here, and that was all I needed.

CHAPTER THIRTEEN

With the first tinge of morning creeping through the window, hinting at a beautifully sunny day, it was easy to forget that it was Thanksgiving. Especially with Logan beside me, my body tucked along his, my hand exploring the far side of his torso, tracing the soft ridges of muscles down to his boxers and up again. I could almost envision the ink beneath my fingertips, dancing as the muscles shifted with each breath and twitch.

We could spend the whole day like this. The whole weekend, really. We both had off, they were calling for nice brisk autumn weather, and there were a thousand things we could do. Some of them even involved leaving bed.

Unfortunately, I had made a promise to several people.

"I still think giving them a little more notice would be better," Logan said, rubbing his fingers through my hair.

"No, that'll give them too much time to dwell on it. And it's harder to hate someone face-to-face. If they see me and remember I'm their son, then they'll take it better," I insisted. Maybe I was right. Or maybe I was chickenshit and putting off revealing the truth as long as possible. I couldn't tell. "Plus Sue will be there, so she can immediately run interference and calm them down if there's a problem."

"She could do that when she got there today if you called them first." He sighed. "But I see your point, and I trust you to know your own family." His hand trailed down my neck, following the slink of my spine. "And you're sure about this?"

That was a trick question. I was sure I wanted to keep Logan with me for always, and that required telling my parents, if only because I wouldn't keep him a secret any longer. I was sure I was tired of having to listen to my mom harp on me about finding someone, when I had someone waiting for me at home.

I was also very sure that I didn't want to have to tell them. A huge part of me had wanted to send them an email with a picture of the two of us, saying he was my boyfriend and I was gay and I'd be bringing him for Thanksgiving. I hadn't, though, for the same reasons I hadn't called.

It was a little late to do it now. Especially since Mom and Dad only checked their email every few days and it wasn't likely they'd see it in time. Of course, I'd had nearly a month to do it and I hadn't, so chances were I wouldn't have done it now either.

Logan gave my hip a squeeze. "Your silence is worrying me."

I sighed and squirmed up to kiss him squarely on the mouth. "I'm sure. I'm terrified and going to second-guess myself until the words come out my mouth, but I'm also absolutely sure."

He held me close for a soft kiss. "You're a walking contradiction."

I returned it and then rolled from his arms. As I sat, my heart was already fluttering in my chest at the thought of today. "I don't want to do this, but I want it done. So I'm sure. Isn't there a quote about that? Bravery means being afraid but doing it anyway?"

He sat with me, the sheets dropping to pile around his waist, the cool air throwing goose bumps across his skin and twisting his nipples into tempting peaks. I was distracted by them until his hand slid along my jaw, tilting my head up to meet his gaze and his kiss. "You are brave, and I'm proud of you. I love you."

"I love you too. Okay, now we need to get up or I'm going to hide under the covers all day."

His chuckle was deep and dirty and in no way discouraging me from doing just that, but he still got out of bed. "I'll hit the shower first, then?"

I was a few seconds back, trapped in that throaty noise, so it took a moment for me to say, "Yeah, sure."

He was gone from the room by the time I got out of bed and shuffled through my closet to decide what to wear. I'd selected a rust-orange shirt and gray jeans that almost passed for slacks and was laying them on the bed when it occurred to me that my amazing, and hot, boyfriend was currently in the shower, about to face what was likely going to be a shitty day. And he was doing it for me.

That deserved a reward.

Clothes abandoned, I headed to the bathroom.

"I'll be done in a few minutes," Logan said when I opened the door.

"Take your time." I let my boxers slip to the floor and drew back the curtain enough to step into the shower with him.

He leaned his head out from under the spray of water and wiped his face off, blinking against the droplets dripping from his hair. It had gotten longer in the past eleven months, though still not shaggy. I pushed it back from his brow, and if that meant I had to step close to him, our naked bodies almost brushing, then that was what had to be done.

He smiled. "Joining me?"

I flashed my own grin. "Nope."

I sank down, crouched with my butt on my heels and his glorious cock in front of my face, already awakening with interest. It was beautiful. Not some perfect porn-star cock—whatever that meant—but real and curved to the left and mine for the taking. So I did, sucking in the head between my lips and greeting the tip with my tongue.

He tasted clean, of water and a touch of soap, but taking him deep, I could still capture a hint of his own personal musk, a little salty, a bit smoky, and filling my mouth to its limit. As the head of his cock nudged the back of my mouth, nearly lodging in my throat, his fingers dug into my hair and clenched. "Jesus fuck," he whispered.

I slurped off, being intentionally noisy, knowing the strange vibrations would tease all along his shaft. Judging by the way his fingers were massaging my scalp, I wasn't wrong. I stopped with my lips around the flared head, taking some time to explore. Running my tongue over the slit, I could already taste the first hint of pre-come, and I wanted more. I teased along the crown, slipping under to the sensitive band of tissue and rubbing.

The only warning I got was a growl. His cock was pulled from my mouth with a sloppy *pop*, and he grabbed me under my arms and hoisted me to my feet. I barely had a moment to regain my balance before I was pinned to the bathroom wall. The tile was cold against my back, but my shiver was from the hunger in his eyes. He cupped my head with one hand a moment before he kissed me so hard my head slammed back, only to be cushioned from the tiles by his palm.

I groaned as his tongue thrust into my mouth and his body pressed against me: straining cock slipping against mine, hips locking me in place. Squirming, I struggled simply to feel the slick, hot skin covering me. A blanket of power. I spread my legs as much as I could while still caged by him, and broke the kiss, my breaths coming in water-saturated pants. "This wasn't the plan."

"Oh?" He nipped at my bottom lip and ground his cock against me. "What was the plan?"

"A blowjob." I nipped back. "To show how grateful I am for today."

"Yeah?" His hands slid down my body, following the curve of the trailing water until his fingers swooped under my ass cheeks and tugged so that our bodies rocked together. "What if I want to show you how grateful I am too?"

I arched my hips toward his, resting my head against the wall and half closing my eyes. "You have my attention."

"Do I?" He tugged again, but this time with force, picking me up. I gasped and spread my legs as I was lifted, and wrapped them around his hips, clinging. My eyes were open now, staring into his, my heart pounding. His grin would have been terrifying if I didn't know him like I did. He growled, "Now I have your attention."

"Yeah? But what about lube?"

It must have been the acoustics in the bathroom, because his chuckle sounded like the devil himself was all around me. It shouldn't have made me thrust against him wantonly, but it did.

His one hand tightened on my ass, and the other buried itself in my hair again. "Hold on."

I wrapped my arms around his shoulders and squeezed my legs, so when he pulled away from the wall, I came with him. He turned us and slammed me against the back wall, out of the shower spray and setting us next to a cheap plastic shelving cabinet. I was barely aware of it. My breath was punched from my lungs as my head bumped against his hand and his fingers gripped my ass cheek.

When I could breathe again, I groaned and dug my blunt nails into his back. "Yeah? What are you gonna do with me now?"

I should have known better than to egg him on, but when he had me like this, I couldn't seem to help myself.

The hand in my hair left, but all I saw were his dark eyes, not where the hand went. "Maybe I should fuck you without any lube." He nipped my lip again. "Tight around my cock." He shoved two fingers in.

I howled—in pain, in pleasure, maybe in fucking need as his words tricked my brain into thinking he was giving me exactly what he'd promised. I clamped around his lubed fingers as he worked them into me, fucking me hard. As the initial wave of shock wore off, heat flared to life and tore through my body.

"Oh, fuck me," I moaned, beginning to shove myself down onto his fingers, wanting them deeper.

Logan chuckled. God, I loved his chuckles. "My pleasure."

The fingers left me, I heard the squirt of the lube bottle, and then after some fumbling, he hoisted me a bit higher on the wall. I caught his gaze and nodded that I was ready. A moment later, the head of his cock breached my hole, hot lubed skin sliding into me. A shudder of absolute pleasure racked my body. Even after a month of going bare, the newness, the intimacy of feeling him in me like this was amazing.

Once the head passed through the tight ring of muscles, he drew back from the wall far enough that gravity took over, sliding him into me with one smooth, unforgiving motion.

I almost came from that. The ache as he filled me had my head thrown back, and a deep groan pushed from my throat. Balls-deep and I wanted more. I wanted to ride it hard until we were both spent and unable to do anything else for the day but lie in bed.

Instead, the hard wall pressed to my back again and he slowly slid out, his hands on my hips lifting me. He was making a show of it too, going all the way until the crown stretched the ring of muscles, and I could do nothing but take what he gave me. It was exactly what I needed today.

He slammed into me, and I muffled a curse against his shoulder. He didn't give me time to adjust—he was already pulling out, then a second later sliding back in. The muscles beneath my lips flexed and strained while he held me. I opened my mouth to taste the skin—a kiss, a lick.

I bit down hard. He was growling words at me, dirty, filthy promises in revenge for my teeth sinking into his skin, but his cock kept filling me, pounding into me, telling me he was enjoying it as much as I was. I released the bite only so I could breathe—gasp, really—and try to work with his fantastically brutal thrusts as much as I could while pinned to the wall.

Logan growled, "Fuck! You're—"

I kissed him, swallowing words like *tight* and *hot* and *going to come.*

The romance books he always read—and that I might have sampled—would say that the bottom could feel the top's come filling him, but that wasn't quite accurate. I felt his hips stutter, his thrust push in and stay, and I knew he was coming in me. Any specific sensations were probably in my imagination, but that didn't matter. I *knew* it. And then his hand wrapped around my cock and I knew nothing except explosive release.

My orgasm ripped from me, shooting down my spine and out my cock, draining my balls as he kept milking the pleasure from me. I was a trembling, shaking mess by the time he finally stopped, finally eased out of me and set my feet on the ground again. I was clinging to his neck, but he didn't try to move away. Simply stepped back and let the water, made slightly cooler from the time we'd spent away from it, pour over us.

I clung still, as his hands trailed down my crack and wiped away lube and come, my sensitive hole practically quivering at his gentle touches.

"Fuck," I whispered against his shoulder.

"Maybe tonight." He turned, nudging my cheek with his nose until I tilted my head and he could kiss me. "I don't think either of us are up for another round."

I squirmed so his hand fell away from my ass, where he'd been nearly fingering me. "Then you better stop that."

He huffed and kissed my cheek, but left my ass alone. "Taking all the fun out of it."

"Sorry, love, but we do have places to be." I kissed the bite mark I'd left on his shoulder. "You soap while I shampoo."

We fell into the easy business of showering, taking care to touch as much as we could between sudsing and rinsing.

When the water was finally off and we'd grabbed our towels, I spread mine wide along my back and wrapped it around us both. Well, as far as it would go. He slid his arms around my waist and touched his nose to mine.

I bumped our noses. "Thank you for being with me. And for your support today."

"I'm proud to be beside you," he murmured.

We stood there in the steamy air, capturing the peace and holding on for as long as we could.

Eventually, however, we had to dry off, get ready, and begin the drive to my parents' house.

The music was blaring; the traffic was, by the grace of some higher power, not bad; and, despite what I was about to do, I was feeling good and loose. The shower fuck had likely played a role in that, but I was trying not to think about shower fucks and my family in the same half an hour. But right now? Feeling great.

So that, of course, was when it happened.

My phone vibrated in the cupholder. Logan glanced over from where he was driving. We were in my car, but he'd offered to drive, probably knowing my attention wouldn't be on the road. "That mine?"

"No, mine." I turned down the music before glancing at the screen. I frowned. "My sister."

I answered the call. "What's up?"

"I'm sorry," she growled down the line like she was using a voice manipulator. "I'm so sorry."

"Sue? What's wrong? You sound weird."

"I'm—" She broke off with a hacking cough that dominoed into several more. "Sorry."

"Shit, are you okay?"

"Sick," she grunted. "I've been tired all week, but last night my nose started running and today . . ." She gave a death cry. Yeah, she sounded it.

"Well, I hope you feel better soon."

"Zacky, I'm sorry."

"Why? Did you get sick on purpose?" I teased.

"No—" pause for coughing "—but I'm not going to be able to be there today."

Oh. Oh shit.

She wasn't going to be there. I had told her—warned her—that I was bringing Logan and I was coming out to Mom and Dad. She was supposed to be there to talk them down if they flipped out about it. Not that I blamed her for being sick! But fuck.

"I'm sorry," she croaked.

"Oh hell, Sue, don't apologize! I'm sorry you're feeling so sick. You focus on feeling better. Do you have someone to help you?" Maybe we could skip Mom and Dad's and use going to help Sue as an excuse.

"Yeah, Judi is coming over. Her husband's overseas and her family is on the other side of the country, so she was going to be on her own anyway." Sue paused for an inhale, and it set off a series of choking coughs.

"I'm glad you won't be alone. Do you need me to come over anyway?"

"No, I'll be fine. Mom will kill you if you bail too."

Damn, there went that escape. "You're not bailing!"

She gave a phlegmy chuckle. "She wasn't convinced I didn't get sick just to ruin her holiday."

"Yes, because everyone loves ruining a four-day weekend by being sick. God, our parents. Well, I hope you feel better soon. And if you need anything, let me know."

"I will."

It was obvious how this short call had drained her energy, so we said our goodbyes and hung up.

"What's happening?" Logan asked. "Is Sue okay?"

"No, she has a horrible cold, it sounds like. So she won't be there today."

"Shit."

Yeah, that was about the long and short of it. I stared down at my phone, suddenly not sure. This seemed like a sign. A warning. Maybe I wasn't meant to tell my parents now, after all.

But we were already three-quarters of the way there, which meant we either had to turn around to return Logan to my place—and I'd have to deal with my parents solo, after having arrived late—or I had to make up a good excuse as to why my sister's ex-boyfriend was coming with me to Thanksgiving dinner.

Honestly, while I had no issue lying to my parents, I had major issues claiming Logan was anything less than the love of my fucking life, especially right in front of him.

So there was only one thing to do.

"Want to turn around?" Logan asked.

"No."

He glanced to me, confusion painted over his brow. "No?" He looked back to the road. "I guess it makes more sense for me to hang out at a diner or something down there. Then you won't be late."

"No."

"Then how are we explaining me being there?"

I took a deep breath. "By telling them you're my boyfriend."

"But your sister won't—"

"I know. I know, but I want to do this. I want to move in together and *be* together everywhere. I don't want to lie to my parents anymore."

He reached over with one hand and grabbed mine, holding it tightly. "You don't have to. I shouldn't have held moving in together over your head like that. It was stupid. You don't need to do this. We can move in anytime."

I squeezed his hand, then lifted it to kiss his knuckles. "Thank you, that means a lot. But I think it's time. No, I know it's time. I choose you over them if they can't accept me for who I am."

"Okay." He didn't sound certain—in fact, he sounded scared—but strangely I felt sure enough for both of us.

The rest of the drive was quiet. I took a little time to text Sue that we were following through with our plans to tell Mom and Dad, so she might need to do some cleanup still. She wished me good luck and told me she'd be there to talk if I needed her.

Before I knew it, we were pulling into the driveway and Logan was turning off the car.

"Last chance," he said. "I don't need to come in." He gave me an approximation of a smile. "I can drive home and start moving your stuff into my place."

I unhooked my seat belt, leaned over, and kissed the corner of his mouth. "Come in and meet my family? Unless you've changed your mind."

"No." He cupped my cheek and kissed me proper. "I love you. Let's do this."

We grabbed the fruit salad and apple pie—my mom only ever baked pumpkin, but my dad loved apple, so we were hoping it would soften him up—and went to the front door. Logan paused, raising his hand to knock, but I just twisted the doorknob and stepped inside, giving him a playful side-eye. "Mom, Dad, we're here!"

"Hi, honey! We're in the kitchen!"

As if my mother would be anywhere else on a holiday morning.

I glanced over at Logan. "Ready?"

He nodded. "You?"

I nodded. As ready as I'd ever be. I wished that Sue could be here, but wishes were like ponies: I didn't have room for them in my life.

We headed down the hallway to the kitchen, Logan trailing slightly behind me. He stopped in the archway, and I continued forward.

"Hey, Mom. We brought the fruit salad you wanted." I set the pie down next to the one that was cooling on the counter, so I could give her a one-armed side-hug. "And, Dad, we made an apple pie, since I know how much you like them."

My mom smiled but didn't turn from what she was doing. "Good! Put the fruit in the fridge, dear. I'll be a minute with these potatoes, then I can say hi properly."

Dad looked up from the newspaper as I popped the container of chopped fruit into the fridge. His eyes gleamed with interest. "Apple pie?"

I grinned at him. "Yep. And Mom has ice cream for dessert to go with it."

"I'll have to thank your little lady for doing that."

Before I could reply, my dad's eyes tracked across the kitchen, following my trail to where "my little lady" would likely be standing. Of course all he found was Logan, who stood up straighter where he was not-quite-hiding, his periwinkle-blue long-sleeved shirt pulling taut across his shoulders.

My dad frowned, his brow scrunching.

Logan briefly caught my eye, but my reactions were delayed, like I was moving through tar. Thankfully Logan was always quick on his feet. "Actually, Mr. Landes, Isaac helped me make the pie."

"Oh," Dad grunted.

Mom spun on her heels, the flap of the apron flaring slightly as if to show how dramatic the moment was.

"Oh!" she squeaked. "Oh, hello, um, Logan. We weren't expecting you."

"I told you I was bringing a guest, Mom," I managed to say, closing the fridge door. I began making my way across the kitchen, but it suddenly seemed larger than the Sahara Desert.

"Well, yes." She tittered. "But when you said a guest, we assumed you meant a girlfriend."

And so the moment arrived. I felt no more prepared for it now than I had in the months—years—of contemplating it. But Logan's warm gaze was on me, giving me strength. So fuck it.

"Well, Logan's my boyfriend."

There. I'd said it. Yet I should have known it wouldn't be that easy.

"Obviously." Mom tittered again. "We thought you were bringing someone special, though, honey." She smiled apologetically at Logan. "Not that you're not welcome."

Which seemed kind of rude even if he hadn't been my boyfriend, but I barely had that thought before words were spilling from my mouth. "Mom, he is special. We're dating. He's my boyfriend. I'm gay."

I stopped short of saying *He fucked me in the shower this morning*, hoping that she'd get the point without me having to be quite so graphic. Also, I didn't want to taint this morning's memories by dragging them through this bullshit.

"Oh."

A heavy hush weighed down the air, making my movements slower as I crossed the kitchen, but I eventually reached Logan, who was standing just inside the kitchen. I clasped his hand, weaving our fingers together to give a visual of what *boyfriend* and *gay* meant. My heart pounded in the space between our palms, but Mom and Dad were silent. Mom was staring at us, her lips parted, eyes wide, confusion on her face, like I'd tried to explain complex physics to her rather than my relationship.

A glance at my father showed very different emotions gathering on his brow. He was visibly in shock, but I could see the anger brewing. The wrinkles on his forehead increased with each breath that I struggled to gasp.

Finally, I couldn't take it any longer.

"I hope we're both still welcome at your table for Thanksgiving. I know this is a bit of a shock, so if you need time to think it through, we can step out. Or if you have questions, we can answer them."

"Questions?" Dad nearly growled. The scrape of the chair legs against the tile pierced the air when he stood. "Yeah, I have a question: when did my son become a goddamn fag?"

I had never heard that word come from my father's mouth before, and it shocked me to hear it now, more than the pure vehemence with which it was said. It must have startled Mom as well, because her face transformed from gaping fish into a frown. "Now, dear, there's no need to name-call. I'm sure—I'm sure we misunderstood what Isaac meant."

The denial was strong with this one. I wasn't about to give a demonstration on what exactly I meant by *This is my boyfriend*, though. I didn't even want to risk a kiss, mostly because my father clearly had no misconception about what I'd said and was glaring at us and moving forward with robotic, jerky motions.

"No, Mom, Dad's right. I'm a fag." I fought the revulsion that wanted to run through my body at the word. Logan squeezed my hand. "Logan's my boyfriend. I love him. I wanted you to know."

And to accept it.

I wasn't sure I'd ever considered that a possibility, though.

"What did you do to my son, you goddamn spic!"

It wasn't really a question, and considering the chair my father had picked up and was swinging at Logan, there was no expectation of an answer.

"No!" I lunged forward, turning my back on my father and throwing my body between Logan and the chair.

In that split second, my only thought was that I hadn't expected violence from my father. Not like this.

As the chair slammed into me, I realized that maybe I should have.

Pain stabbed my body as the legs hit me. *Crack! Crack!* I was shoved forward into Logan, who caught me before I fell. I clung to his broad shoulders, fingers twisting in his shirt. I stared at his chin. *What's happening? Is this happening?*

"You're disgusting!" my dad shouted.

The chair slammed into me again, but this time there were no legs to break off and nowhere for the momentum to push me except into Logan, plastering my face to his chest. Hot pain splintered through my body.

Logan stepped back, dragging me with him. "What the fuck!"

"No!" That was my mom.

I heard noises behind, but all I could focus on was the button poking into my cheek. It didn't particularly hurt, but all my attention narrowed in on that. It wasn't pleasant. I should move. Adjust myself so I could lie in Logan's arms more comfortably. But I couldn't seem to. Why was I lying in Logan's arms if I was standing up? Was I standing up?

"Zack? Zack? Fuck, c'mon, babe." Logan sounded fragile. Scared.

I wanted to tell him it was fine. My dad would calm down, and we'd talk this through. Instead I clung to Logan, vaguely aware that we were walking—well, he was walking and my feet were taking me wherever he led. The cool air was refreshing on my face. Oh, I was no longer pressed against his chest. I blinked into the sunlight and my feet faltered, but Logan was there to steady me. I looked over.

Logan's face was pasty like uncooked wheat bread, and his eyes were wide, framing the irises in white. "Zack?"

"Ouch."

A laugh startled out of him: a short, humorless bark. "Yeah, babe. We're gonna go to the hospital and get that checked out."

Get what checked out? I wanted to ask, but everything hurt. Obviously something needed to get treated. "Okay."

He got me in the car and—ouch—gingerly strapped the seat belt over me. I closed my eyes and rested my head back. Ouch.

My car purred to life and a cheery pop song blared from the radio, then was immediately silenced. I could hear Logan's heavy breathing over the engine.

"It's going to be okay," I said.

"He hit you with a goddamn chair." Logan's breath hitched. The car began to move.

"I couldn't let him hit you with it."

"Not the fucking point." Another hitched breath. "How are you doing over there?"

I didn't want to think about it, because thinking about it made me aware of the pain. All along my back, and my head. Something warm was trickling down my neck, and I had a feeling I knew what it was.

"My name is Isaac Landes, and it's Thanksgiving Day. My chest hurts," I added as talking made me realize how much. I focused on taking shallow breaths.

"How are you doing over there?"

We'd stopped moving. I forced my eyes open to squint at him. "You just asked me that."

He grimaced. "Let's get you inside."

He trotted around the front of the car and helped me get out. We were at the hospital ER entrance, which didn't make sense since the hospital was ten minutes away from my parents' house. And how did Logan know how to get here?

Inside I was dizzied by the blinding lights. I vaguely heard Logan say *attacked with a chair* and *disoriented*. He must have said some other magical words, because we were immediately taken back to a little space sectioned off with curtains. It was the shortest time I'd ever waited in an ER.

"I'll be back," Logan was saying, lips touching my temple as he helped me settle on the bed. "I need to move the car, but I'll be right back. The nurses will take care of you."

"Okay."

I blinked and something tugged on my scalp. I lifted my hand to swat it away, but a hand was holding my wrist. "What's that?"

"Finishing up the stitches," a high-pitched voice said behind me.

"Stitches? Why do I need stitches? Why do I hurt?"

"It's okay, babe," Logan said, and my eyes tracked to where he was sitting in front of me. He was holding my wrists.

"Hurting is not okay."

His smile was a shattered, broken thing. He swallowed, but seemed to struggle to do that simple action. "No, it's not. But the doctor's going to give you meds to hurt less, okay?"

"Okay."

Logan squeezed my wrists, and I took comfort in the strength there. I closed my eyes.

"How long will the confusion last?"

"It varies person to person," a new voice said. I opened my eyes to see a woman with a tablet in hand. The lights were nicely dimmed. "Once his body has a chance to rest and heal, he'll likely feel better and be less confused. He probably won't remember much of today, but the concussion is mild. You have the sheet with the signs to watch for."

"And he'll be okay for a long drive home?"

"That should be fine."

I closed my eyes.

"How are you doing?" Logan asked.

I opened my eyes. The car was vibrating around me and my head felt like cotton set on fire. The world was flying by. There was the pain beneath the sweet bliss of the drugs, and I was very careful not to move more than necessary. I slowly turned my head. Logan was staring straight forward, hands gripping the wheel with murderous intent. I swallowed a dry mouthful and broke the seal on my crusty lips with my tongue. "Thirsty."

He took a deep breath, let out a long exhale, then picked up a water bottle from the cupholder and held it closer for me. "Think you can drink?"

"Yeah." My fingers ached as I wrapped them around the bottle, but I was able to lift it to my lips and pour the cool, refreshing water into my mouth. Swallowing was heaven. "Thanks."

"How do you feel otherwise?"

"Shitty. We were just in the hospital, weren't we?"

"Uh-huh. We'll be home soon."

I wondered if he had teleported us there, because the drive from the hospital to my place should have taken longer. Unless we'd been at the hospital by me, but then how had he gotten *there* so fast?

"You slept through most of the drive," Logan answered. I must have said some of that aloud.

"Oh."

"Don't worry, the doctor said you'd feel better tomorrow."

"She said I probably would," I corrected.

His laugh was wet and choked. "You're right, she did."

I sighed, took another sip of water, then tucked the bottle between my legs and closed my eyes.

CHAPTER FOURTEEN

The next morning I woke in pain. It hit me like a goddamn chair to the back, along with the realization that my father had hit me with a goddamn chair to the back.

I groaned and tried to roll over to give my neck, kinked from having slept on my stomach all night, some relief, but the heavy weight of Logan's arm held me still. Which, after my slight struggle to move and the resulting pain that flared down my back, I was grateful for. Moving was a terrible idea.

I manfully didn't whimper. Much.

"Shh, babe, shh." Logan's voice was gruff; I'd likely woken him. He sat up slowly, as if afraid to jostle the bed, and kept his hand on my hip. "How you doing?"

The question sounded so brittle. Maybe he was afraid of the answer. I certainly wasn't too wild about it myself. I blinked a few more times, and my newly awake brain tried to shuffle all of yesterday's events. It was harder than I would have liked. "For getting hit with a chair? Pretty okay."

The chuckle that followed was low and sad, but it came with a kiss to my shoulder. "You remember that, then?"

"Yeah. And some of the hospital. But that's fuzzy. My body sort of aches all over." I tried for humor to make this whole thing less sucky. "Kinda like when we did that fucking marathon after running ten miles."

"Not our best decision," Logan admitted. "But that's not too bad. Maybe we can sit you up and see how your head is?"

"Do I have a concussion?"

"A mild one. They weren't worried: your scans were clean. You were responsive through the night when I checked on you, but they said you'd probably be dizzy for a few days."

"Okay." I shifted my body, trying to assess how bad everything hurt. I could feel a few bits tugging unnaturally, and I wondered if I had stitches. As quickly as the thought came, it left. I focused on getting my arms under me, pushing myself up—I was going to trust that Logan's implied command not to roll over was for the best—and then twisting so I was sitting.

I realized a few facts: it was still dark out, dizziness was in fact a thing, and I was wearing my favorite pair of sweats. I didn't remember putting them on, and it warmed my heart to imagine Logan caring for me after the shit-fest that was yesterday.

"How do you feel?"

I closed my eyes and took a deep breath, waiting for the listing room to settle. Everyone on TV always described it as spinning, but it felt more like I was aboard a boat on rocky seas. Not that I'd ever been on such a boat, but this was exactly how I imagined it would feel. Only drier.

"Hun?"

"Sorry. Yes, I'm dizzy, but it's passing." I opened my eyes to prove to him I was okay. My eyes tracked to the alarm clock and the ungodly hour that was meant for business executives who commuted an hour but not for two guys who had the day off. "I'm sorry I woke you."

"Jesus, Isaac, you don't need to apologize for that."

"But you had a long day taking care of me—you're probably tired."

"Yeah, and your goddamn father put you in the hospital, so I think you're allowed a few things," he growled. After visibly taking a deep breath, he leaned over and kissed my bare shoulder. "Are you hungry? Need some Tylenol? A foot massage? A blowjob? Whatever you want is yours."

I looked over at him—slowly—and smiled. "I'll say yes to the Tylenol. And food, though I don't think I'm quite awake for that. I'll hold off on the blowjob." I tilted forward and kissed him. "Thank you for taking care of me. But can you tell me everything—what happened? How bad is it?"

His grimace told me more than enough, but hearing yesterday described was still difficult. Partially because remembering the damn chair hitting me made shocks of pain run down my back, but mostly because it meant remembering the horror on my mother's face and the rage on my father's. Part of me was bitter and smug, hissing *I knew it*, but too much of me had hoped that it wouldn't turn out the way it had. There was no joy in gloating.

"Nothing broken or damaged, thankfully," Logan said, and swallowed hard. "A dozen stitches overall where shards hit you, but they're the dissolving kind, so no follow-up unless there's issues. The doctor said the concussion is mild, and the scans were clear, but she gave us a list of things to watch for. That means when I ask how you feel, you tell it to me straight, got it?"

"Straight as I can."

He kissed my shoulder again. "Yeah, yeah. I still wish I could've punched his face in."

"Logan."

"I know, I know. But I don't care if he's your dad. We should still report his abusive ass to the police. Assault and battery of his own son. Who knows what he'd do to someone else's. What that bigoted asshole would have done to me."

I winced and tilted away from him. I couldn't remember having this argument last night, but I instinctually knew that we had, which was, frankly, terrifying. I took as deep a breath as my aching body allowed, then slowly released it. I *should* report the attack, make my dad realize what he'd done was wrong, but I couldn't. He was my father. Even if he didn't think I was good enough to be his son, I still loved him. Even knowing he would have hurt Logan . . . I could only be happy he hadn't.

Beside me, Logan sighed. "Guess it was too much to hope you'd change your mind in the morning. You were pretty adamant about not doing it last night too."

"I'm sorry?"

"It's your choice." It sounded like it took all of Logan's gritted teeth to say, but he'd said it. "If he harms a single hair on your body again, though, I'm going to beat him to a pulp."

"That's fair."

"I'm glad you're being reasonable about that." Logan's laugh was about as carefree as I could expect this morning. It radiated through me like magic, and I imagined it healing all my aches.

I smiled and listed toward him. "Well, at least we can move in together now."

"Yeah." Logan frowned and looked down. He reached out and clasped my hand, holding it tight. For a moment I waited, wondering if he was going to explain the blatantly unenthusiastic response. Abruptly he raised his head. "Hey, are you hungry?"

I blinked in surprise. Hungry? Why was he asking if I was hungry?

That quick, I could feel my grip on my previous concerns slipping away.

"Yeah, I could eat."

"You want breakfast in bed?"

I shifted on the soft mattress and considered needing to be propped up by a dozen fluffy pillows. The thought made my spine ache. "Uh, better go for the kitchen table."

"Your wish is my command. Wait," he added when I moved to throw back the covers to stand. "Let me be there just in case."

I thought he was being silly, but I humored him anyway, pushing back the covers and putting my feet on the floor to wait while he got out of bed and came around to my side.

"Ready?"

"I was ready a minute ago."

He held out his arms, offering a ring of support should I lose my balance, presumably. "Glad to see your sarcasm wasn't damaged."

"You'll have to pry it from my cold dead hands," I said, rising to my feet.

I swayed, but he didn't immediately grab me, letting me steady myself and wait for the dizziness to pass. Only then did he wrap his arms around me and draw me to his chest. He set a kiss on my crown. "How about we let you keep it, then?"

"Sounds good." I nodded against his chest, closing my eyes as his heat and scent surrounded me. If I hadn't hurt so much, and been so very aware of how delicately his arms were touching my back, I would have been turned on. As it was, I felt protected. Safe from all of yesterday's shit. I could have stayed there forever.

Moving must have woken my body up, though, because my stomach grumbled its complaint at being empty. Really empty.

"When did I last eat?"

His fingers slid as light as droplets over my skin. "I fed you when we got home, though you weren't too hungry. C'mon."

He got me situated at the kitchen table with an extra cushion on the seat, even though my butt was fine, and a pillow between me and the backrest, in case I leaned on it. I didn't mind the fussing, although I was sort of waiting for the bubble wrap to come out.

He handed me my phone before he set to cooking, so I could answer the texts I'd received last night—he'd wisely taken my phone away before I'd done the concussion equivalent of drunk texting—and update my friends on my big "coming out." There were a few messages in the group chat asking how it had gone, then a few fretting before Jenna sent, *Logan said you're OK and will give us an update tomorrow :(Love you! Hope everything's okay!*

I smiled and typed, *I'm OK considering. My parents didn't take it well and my dad attacked me. Logan and I spent yesterday in the hospital. I have a MILD concussion, some stitches, and bruises. But overall I'm fine. Logan's making me breakfast now.*

After I'd sent the message, I remembered it was fuck early in the morning on Black Friday and, aside from Emmett and Jackson, who would likely be awoken by their daughter, everyone would be asleep. Well, that gave me more time to find my feet before I got a flood of responses. I put my phone to sleep and leaned back—gingerly—on the pillow. It pressed on my lower back and wasn't too bad. My eyes tracked to Logan fussing at the stove, and I smiled.

"What's for breakfast?"

"Toast and eggs with coffee and orange juice."

"Not French toast? Pancakes? Waffles?" I teased.

He glanced over his shoulder at me. "I can if you want, but I know how much you love eggs, and I figured this would be fast."

"It sounds great. Though I am having an odd craving for pancakes."

Logan chuckled and turned his gaze back to the eggs. "We can do those for dinner, if you want."

My whims seemed to be the order for the day. After breakfast—and a dose of painkillers—we returned to bed for a few more hours until it was reasonable. Then he took me into the shower for the most gentle shower sudsing imaginable. If I hadn't known raucous amounts of sex were off the table—trust me, they were—I would have thought he was buttering me up. In reality I just wasn't supposed to get my stitches too wet or soapy, and it gave Logan an excuse to examine every inch of my injuries, which he did.

He was probably blaming himself for them, but he didn't say anything and I didn't have the energy to push. We could talk about it later, when my head didn't pound every time the drugs wore off and moving too fast didn't result in grabbing something for balance.

After a thorough toweling off, I wandered back to the kitchen to get my phone. My friends had all woken up.

Emmett: *Holy fuck. What did he do?*

Jackson: *Oh no :(*

Mark: *Fuck, are you okay?*

Jenna: *Did you get the police involved?*

Laura: *<3 *hugs**

Roe sent a GIF of someone wrapping a child in bubble wrap.

I loved my friends, although I knew they weren't going to be wild about my answer to Jenna's question. I updated them on how I was (*OK. Sore and not pretty, but Logan is taking care of me*), what my dad had done (*slammed a chair against my back as he was attacking Logan*), and if I had told the police (*no*).

Jenna: *Why the fuck not?*

Wow, she was fast.

Laura: *What my lovely lady means is, why didn't you report him? That's scary. You had to go to the hospital! He shouldn't get away with it.*

So I told them the same thing I'd told Logan, knowing they'd take it about as well.

Isaac: *He's my dad and I love him, even if he doesn't love me. I don't want to put him through that.*

Roe: *That's a shitty reason. He obviously had no issue putting you through that.*

Isaac: *He was aiming at Logan.*

Jenna: *Then no offense but I wish you hadn't stepped in, because Logan has the sense to report his assaulting ass to the police.*

Roe: *Also, he's ripped, it probably wouldn't have hurt much.*

I didn't want to keep arguing, so instead I replied, *Are you saying I'm feeble?*

Roe: *No, I'm saying if it was me, I'd be a pancake on the floor.*

Isaac: *Good save :p*

Roe: *I'm glad you're okay. Is there anything we can do for you?*

Logan came into the kitchen, stopping to kiss my temple before he headed to the counter to start making tea. I smiled up at him and told my friends, *Logan has everything covered. I think I'm good. Thanks.*

"You're going to spoil me," I told Logan.

"Good." He set out two mugs with tea bags while the water heated. The fox on his stared at me cheerfully. "I still can't believe yesterday happened. I never should have—"

"I told you, I wanted to do it."

"I know, but I—"

This time my ringing phone interrupted him. I glanced down. "Oh, it's Sue. I should take this." I hit Answer and raised it to my ear. "He—"

"Zacky!" Croaked over the line, followed by a fit of coughs. I waited for her to get back under control, keeping the phone slightly away from my ear. When she finally settled, she said, more softly now, "Mom called me. Are you okay? What really happened?"

"I'll survive. Nothing that won't heal. And what do you mean 'What really happened?' I thought Mom called."

"Yeah, and she said that you told them and Dad called you both fags"—I could hear her wince—"and Logan tried to attack them, and

Dad went to fend him off with a chair and you somehow got hit, and then Logan threw you over his shoulder and ran off with you."

What the actual fuck? "That's not what happened."

"I figured," Sue said harshly. "That's why I wanted you to tell me."

"I told them, and Dad fucking attacked Logan with a chair, and I jumped in front of him—"

"My hero!" Logan called loud enough for Sue to hear. He sounded teasing, but there was sap-filled worship in his eyes.

"Anyway. Dad hit me—twice—and Logan *gently* led me out and took me to the hospital. Concussion and a few stitches. Not bad, considering. I can't believe she told you those lies."

Sue sighed. "It's possible that's how she remembers it happening. I told her I didn't believe either of you would do that, and then she started simpering about how I'd known and not told them and they could have done something if they'd known—fuck knows what they would have done—and I told her if you and Logan weren't welcome in their house, then I wasn't going to be coming over either. I got your back, Zacky."

Tender warmth flooded me, and I wished Sue were here so I could wrap her in a tight hug. Then she started coughing and my back twinged, reminding me that hugs weren't going to be tight for a while, and I reevaluated the benefits of doing this over the phone.

"Thanks, Sue." I hesitated, guilt beginning to taint the warmth. "But I don't want you to lose all your family too."

"Don't," she rasped, then cleared her throat. "You are my family. And besides, Dominic's family is already trying to adopt me, if how they're taking care of me is any indication."

"Who's Dominic?"

"Oh. Um. My new boyfriend."

"You didn't tell me!"

"It got intense super fast and I didn't want to jinx it. It's pretty new." She sounded almost meek. Well, as meek as Sue ever got.

"Yet you've met his family?" I couldn't help teasing.

"They're local. When I got sick, Dom was over taking care of me and he told his mother, who then brought soup, and then the sisters took turns when Dom was at work, and I think I've met like half his family now. They're all very nice."

She sounded in love. Not only with this Dominic, but his entire family. I smiled on her behalf and hoped it would work out. "I'm glad to hear, but I don't want you to feel obligated to cut Mom and Dad out of your life because of me."

A snort, followed by a hacking cough, came over the line. "Zack, family is about love, and if they can't accept you, then I can't love them. I love you."

"I love you too," I choked out around the sudden lump in my throat.

"Then that's all we need. We've got each other and all our friends. Fuck Mom and Dad and their small-minded, bigoted, old-fashioned, horrible attitudes."

"You're the best sister in the world."

Her laugh was soft and weak. "And you're the best brother in the world. And I hate to do this, but getting all fired up has exhausted me."

"Go rest and get well."

"You too."

We said our goodbyes and hung up. The joy in my chest from her support was still tainted by the guilt that I'd made her choose between me and our parents, but I tried not to let it overwhelm me. It was her choice, just like I'd made mine.

Logan set a cup of tea in front of me, and I grabbed his hand before he went too far. He paused and studied me, a frown creasing his brow. "Everything okay?"

I didn't need to tell him that no, it really wasn't. But I had him here, so I was able to smile up at him and say, "It will be."

153

CHAPTER FIFTEEN

The next two days were a study in being absolutely spoiled. My friends all stopped by to see how I was, sometimes bringing sweets they knew I loved. I tried to tell them I wasn't that bad off and the doting wasn't necessary, but I couldn't help feeling pleased to see them all. It helped to know they'd made sure to visit me, now that my family was out of the picture.

Meanwhile, Logan cooked every meal, and pretty much waited on me hand and foot. I told him he was going overboard, that having him nearby if I needed him was enough, but he insisted, saying it made him feel better about the whole thing. If it eased his guilt—which he didn't need to have—then I wasn't going to argue, especially since nothing I said seemed to convince him.

There was one moment that wasn't so perfect over the long weekend. It was Sunday morning, and we were lying down, cooling from a heated mutual handjob. I felt a little dizzy from the excitement and suddenly landing on my back—not to mention the sharp ache that stabbed in various points there—but none of that could wipe away the buzz from the orgasm.

"You know," I said, euphoric, "now that we can move in together, we can do this every morning."

"Oh. Yeah."

He couldn't have sounded less enthusiastic if I'd asked him to clean an entire Victorian manor top to bottom by himself. I rolled over, more gingerly this time, to face him. He was staring at the ceiling, his lips tugged down.

I shuffled closer and stroked his chest with my fingertips. "You do want to move in together, don't you?"

"Yeah." I opened my mouth to ask what was wrong, but before I could, he rolled onto his side and gripped my chin between his thumb and forefinger, holding me still for a kiss. "Sorry, my brain just realized it's Sunday and we have to go back to work tomorrow. Then I got to thinking that I should drive you in since you probably shouldn't be driving yet."

"I was going to take transit."

His frown deepened. "Maybe on Tuesday. I don't want you dealing with that and a full day of work."

I nodded, unable to argue with that logic, and ducked my head to kiss the fingers that had captured my chin. "Thank you for everything this weekend."

A shadow flitted across his face, and he gently tipped my face up to meet his kiss. "You don't have to thank me for anything. It's the least I could do after what happened." He kissed me again. "I love you."

Warmth spread through me like it always did at those words, and I beamed back at him. "I love you too."

I was feeling pretty good by the time I got together with my friends on Saturday. Logan's friends were playing touch football, and he'd laughingly excused me from the torture since my friends had something planned too. Although if they hadn't, I probably wouldn't have been required to play—neither of us wanted to risk my head being jostled.

Although all my friends had seen me at some point during the last weekend, they fussed over me when I arrived—having driven my own car!—until I'd had enough and batted them away. Eventually the conversation turned to Rosa, or the new show on Netflix, or the video game they were playing. I listened, letting the voices wash over me, glad for the sense of normality it brought with it.

The week had been weird. I'd been on my own—Logan had been distracted and overwhelmed with work—and the apartment had felt oddly quiet. I'd suggested to Logan that I could come over to his place after work, hinting that I could move some stuff in, but he'd said I shouldn't strain myself while I was recovering and he probably wouldn't be much fun anyway.

I'd wanted to tell him that it wasn't about fun—I didn't need him to entertain me—but that I just wanted to be near him. That had sounded desperate, though, even in my head. He'd spent all of the past weekend with me, so I should give him some room, right? Despite the fact we'd previously been talking about moving in together. Maybe that was off the table now? Though I had no idea why it would be.

"Uh-oh, Zack's got a frown on."

I shook my head—gently—and focused on Jenna. "What?"

"Nothing. We seemed to have lost you. What's going on?"

I swallowed. I didn't want to unload all my relationship worries on them. They'd probably think I was being paranoid. Or worse, complaining about what was *maybe* a little wrong when I had something as good as Logan in my life. "Sorry . . . Thinking about last week, I guess."

Everyone's expression transformed into one of sympathy.

"I still can't believe that happened," Mark said, shaking his head from his spot on the floor.

"I can." I touched right next to where the stitches were in my head. "Maybe not this badly."

"It seems hard to believe that one of our parents would attack us," Roe said, putting a hand on my shoulder and gently squeezing. "I'm glad you and Logan got out of there fast."

"Yeah." I sighed. "But that's the thing, isn't it? It wasn't hard for me to believe that my dad would do this. I mean, maybe not with a chair; yelling is his modus operandi. But I knew he'd be angry. It's why I didn't want to tell them. I knew I'd, well, be unwelcome there to say the least."

"Not to be harsh," Laura said, "but if they didn't know about this whole huge part of your life—who you love and want to spend your life with, don't pretend you don't—then were *you* really welcome before?"

I groaned and leaned back on the couch. "That's why I told them. But they're my family. Now I've lost them." The truth had literally been beaten into me, and yet it still hurt to say out loud.

"You have Sue," Jenna reminded.

"I know. She's been great, standing by me through everything. But they're *my family*. I didn't want to lose that." I sagged forward, the weight of everything crushing down on my shoulders, until my elbows were on my knees. "Now I have."

Jackson grunted. "You have us."

"Yeah, but you're not family." I pressed my face to my hands, needing to close my eyes and choke off the emotions that were trying to come up. "It's different."

Silence followed. At first I thought they were all as saddened as I was by my loss, or sad for me about it, but when the silence dragged on longer, I raised my eyes.

Right into Jackson's wide, accusing gaze. His mouth was partially open with shock, but the wrinkle across his brow and the tightness around his eyes spoke of hurt. What had I missed? What was wrong? If he saw the questions in my expression, he didn't answer them.

"What?" I finally asked.

"'Not family'?" Jackson croaked.

"No." I straightened a little, peering around at everyone. No one seemed as aghast as Jackson, but no one looked as confused as I felt either. "You guys are amazing, but you're not family."

Jackson stood abruptly. "Thank fuck for that, I suppose. If we were, we'd be putting you in the hospital too!"

He stormed out, and it was my turn to stare with my jaw dangling in surprise. What the hell had just happened?

"Um?" I turned to my friends, trying to find someone who could explain.

Emmett's lips were twisted as he glanced from the door Jackson had gone through and back to me. I had a feeling if he hadn't had Rosa in his arms, he would have already been with Jackson. Instead he was now glaring at me with pursed lips.

"What?" I repeated.

"We're your family too," Roe said quickly. "Not biological, not like Sue, but we're family."

I shook my head. "No, you guys are my *friends*. You mean the world to me. I chose you. Family is that thing you get stuck with. They've been with you from the beginning, for better or worse."

"Well, we're your *chosen* family, then," Jenna tried.

No. My family—except for Sue—was full of assholes who would rather take a chair to their son than deal with him being gay. My friends were better than that. Meant more than that. I shook my head. "No, you're my *friends*. Don't you see how that's better?"

"Okay, you guys work this out," Emmett said, passing Rosa off to Roe. "I'm going to talk to Jack."

Then Emmett was gone, and everyone else continued to try to explain why they were family. They didn't seem to get that I didn't want them to be family. I mean, I did, because they would be awesome family, but it didn't work that way. I wanted *my* family, blemishes and all. You only got one chance, and mine was done. *Except for Sue*, I had to keep reminding myself, clinging to that one strand of hope.

Because family was always there for you. As wonderful as they were, friends could come and go; there was so little history tying you together. Interests could change, or people could get annoyed with each other, and then you wouldn't be friends anymore. Nothing demanded a connection.

But Sue and I? We hardly had any interests in common, and yet we had our whole childhoods in common. That bound us together in a way my friends didn't seem to get.

Eventually they gave up on trying to get me to see their point—when it was them who didn't get my point—and Roe said I was arguing a matter of semantics and could I agree that everyone loved me and was here for me?

Of course I agreed with that.

"Eeeee!" Rosa confirmed as Emmett and Jackson returned.

With a wan smile, Jackson took Rosa back from Roe and sat on the couch. It didn't escape my notice that he wasn't looking at me, wasn't talking to me. Emmett met my eyes and shrugged, then sat down next to his husband, wrapping a protective arm around Jackson's shoulders.

I wished Logan were here. Obviously I was glad he could hang with his friends and they were getting along now—though their constant fighting proved how fragile friendships were—but I wanted his arms around me while everyone stared at me like I'd taken a dump on the floor. I'd come to see my friends and have fun, to get some of last weekend's stress off my chest, but I seemed to have taken more on instead. I'd lost my family, Logan was being weird, and now my friends were silently brewing that I didn't consider them family. Everything was piling up while all my supports were being washed out from under me. I was drowning on solid ground.

I almost wanted to tell them I did think of them as family, if only so they'd stop being mad. In the end, though, lying seemed a greater sin than our conflict warranted, so I said nothing.

The rest of the day, I barely said a word as conversations swarmed around me, never pulling me in.

CHAPTER SIXTEEN

I knew my friends were still upset with me over the next few days, because our group text chat was oddly silent. Usually it was filled with random thoughts, pictures, or links that we came across throughout the day, but now half of what happened in there was from me.

See, I wanted to tell them, bitterness on the back of my tongue, *this is why you're not family. Family wouldn't break apart over something so small as this. Because family loves you no matter what, because you're bound by blood.*

Well, no matter what, unless you're gay and your parents are homophobes.

I was screwed.

Then I shared my concerns with Logan while he was chopping vegetables for dinner. I was spending most nights at his place, but I hadn't raised the question about moving in together again. I wasn't sure I could face his apathy. Or rejection.

"They're probably busy with things," he said.

"Too busy to text?"

"Didn't you say Roe was freaking out over edits or something for that thing they wrote? And Rosa had a bad cold?"

"Yeah," I mumbled beside him, prodding the steak on the skillet. "But they've all been busy before and it never stopped them."

Logan sighed. "Or it did, but you weren't concerned about it. Now you think there's a reason, so it seems bigger than it is. I'm sure it's nothing."

It's nothing became my mantra for the next week, and it got me through. By the following Thursday, the chat was back to being a bustle of conversation. Thank goodness. They weren't mad; Logan was right and they'd been busy. I felt silly, but at least Logan was the only one who'd witnessed my anxiety.

Then Friday happened.

Jackson: *In some sort of miracle, Rosa's cold is all cleared up! Everyone want to come over for brunch on Saturday morning?*

Jenna: *Laura and I are in!*

Roe: *Sounds good. I'll bring that french toast casserole.*

Mark: *Exactly what I need. I'll be cliche and bring the mimosas.*

I frowned at my phone, wishing this conversation had happened two days ago, although it couldn't have as they'd been waiting for Rosa to feel better. But still. I typed, *Sorry, I can't make that. I promised to go into work and do overtime for this project. What about Sunday?*

Jackson: *Saturday is really better for us. We'll see you next week, I guess.*

I barely saw the flood of texts that followed, my phone pinging constantly in my hand, my screen flashing to life every five seconds.

"We'll see you next week, I guess."

I swallowed as the chat continued moving, and I had to scroll up again to read those words. Again and again. As if I might have misread how easily I'd been dropped. Nope. Every time the words were the same.

"We'll see you next week, I guess."

Eventually I silenced the conversation and opened my texts with Sue.

How are you doing?

It was Friday night, and she probably had plans with her own friends or her boyfriend, but that didn't make the silence that answered me any easier to take.

It's nothing, I tried to tell myself. But the mantra wasn't working. I felt detached—not like an emotionless robot, but like a balloon that had slipped—no, that a child had let go of. I was drifting away on whatever currents wanted to take me, and the child was tearlessly watching me go. Or, worse yet, had already forgotten me.

I shuddered. *It's nothing. It's nothing. It's nothing.*

Yet it certainly felt like something.

I was still sitting on the couch when Logan got home. The mantra had become a faint buzzing in my head, white noise that lulled me into a Zen-like state. The *click* of the door closing snapped me out of it, and then Logan's warm voice said, "Honey, I'm home."

A dry chuckle escaped my chest as I stood and tried to shake off the malaise that weighted my limbs. I didn't want him to know I'd been worrying about my friends again. *It's nothing.* He understood how important friends were, but he also seemed to handle conflict— in general, everything—with a natural ease I couldn't grasp. No need to bog him down with my fretting.

"It's a little weird that I got here before you when you work from home," I said, moving to greet him on the way to the kitchen. He had a bag of groceries in each hand, and I took advantage of his incapacitation to slide my hands up his chest and mold my body to his front. His strength seemed to seep into me. Not like I was stealing it, but like it overflowed from him. I smiled when he leaned down to meet my kiss.

"Good evening to you too. I finished up work early, so I decided to run out and get something special for dinner."

"Oooh? Special?" I took one of the bags, because it was a nice thing to do, but also to peek inside. There was a head of lettuce, a clove of garlic, and a packet of shredded cheese.

"Well, not like super special. But my mom's fish taco recipe." He threw a smile at me over his shoulder as he headed to the kitchen, and the warmth there melted away the last of my earlier tensions.

"That sounds very special to me. I'm excited. Want a hand?" I followed him to the kitchen since I had half the ingredients.

"If you'd like. You can prep the veggies while I cook the fish."

"I hope I don't mess it up."

He grinned as he started pulling out bowls and pans. "It's pretty straightforward. I'm doing the hard part."

"Frying fish?"

"Well," he amended, "I'm doing the *hardest* part. This is a special recipe, but I didn't say it was difficult."

He stuck the recipe to the cabinet with a clip, so it was easy to access as he worked. I glanced over it. "It sounds delicious, and now I want to know why we haven't had it before."

"Mostly because I couldn't find the recipe. And once you've had Mama's, no other recipe will compare."

"Oooh, the challenge is on!"

Working side by side, we put dinner together without much fuss and only a small mess, laughing as the oil spit and hissed and we danced around trying not to get burned. For the first time in what felt like hours, the tension in my shoulders melted away, the knot in my stomach loosened, and I was able to breathe. Once everything was prepared, I set the table while he stacked the finished ingredients into the soft shells. I set out two beers as he brought the food to the table.

"It looks delicious," I said, sitting down.

He bent over and kissed my temple. "It tastes good too. Thank you for your help." He sat across from me, and we filled our plates with tacos.

They tasted even better than they looked. The fish was tender, flaking apart in my mouth and spilling the spiced juices across my tongue. The pico de gallo's flavors accented the fish, and the lettuce added the perfect amount of crunch.

I swallowed the last bite of my third taco and leaned back with a sigh, resting my hand on my happily full stomach. "Thank you, that was exactly what I needed." Later, I'd blame what came out of my mouth next on the immense satisfaction coursing through my veins. Or maybe I needed to feel wanted. Either way, I said, "I'm looking forward to moving in together so we can cook like this more often."

Across the table, Logan stiffened, and guilt shot across his face. If I'd been eating, if I hadn't been watching him, hoping to see warmth in those lovely dark-gray eyes, I would have missed it. But I was watching, and I saw.

That fragile peace I'd found in the past hour shattered.

"You do still want to move in together, right?"

Another hesitation that seemed to stretch between us like the gulf of a desert. That guilt lingered in his eyes. My heart plummeted to my stomach, where it lurched uneasily on the pile of food.

"Never mind." I found myself standing up. The screech of the chair against the tile sent a shiver down my spine.

"Isaac, sit down, it's not . . ." He wet his lips.

I waited and waited, but he didn't finish that thought. Maybe he didn't know how it ended either.

"It's not?" I echoed, trying to gather up the pieces of myself and form them into something that wasn't raw pain. The shape they took was anger. "You never really wanted to move in together, did you? I mean, sure, maybe at the beginning, but not now you've had time to think about it. You made that goddamn stupid rule about me telling my parents before we moved in together so that we wouldn't ever do it. Because you didn't think I'd come out, did you?"

I sucked in a noisy breath, and he reached out, opening his mouth, but I was faster.

"Well, joke's on you." My voice cracked, and I had to swallow down the revulsion swimming up my throat. "But don't worry, I won't demand anything from you that you don't want to give." I stepped away from the table, nearly tripping on the leg in my haste.

"Isaac, it's not like that!"

Spinning toward him, I pinned him with a glare. "Not like *what*? Not like I lost my family *for you* because you *said* we couldn't move in together until I told them? Not like you've been avoiding it ever since? I've seen you, Logan! I mention living together, and you act like you'd cut your leg off to get out of it. You say yes with the reluctance of a torture victim! I don't need a goddamn diagram," I spat. "You already drew me one."

I saw the wincing guilt in his face, and I didn't want to see any more. I didn't think I could. My cobbled-together anger was already beginning to crumble, and I couldn't let him think me pitiful. More pitiful. He'd done nothing but be my strength when I was weak, and he was obviously sick of it. I marched toward the front door.

He followed me to the small foyer. "Isaac, wait! C'mon, let's sit down and talk."

A paraphrase of the old favorite *We need to talk* right before he broke my heart. I shoved my trembling feet into my shoes, clinging to my scraps of anger. "About what? About how I gave up my family for you and I shouldn't have?" Why was I saying that repeatedly? Did I enjoy the painful crevices of guilt on his face that deepened each time I said it? "You don't want to move in together. That's fine." My voice cracked. It wasn't fine at all. "I just need to go home now."

I yanked my jacket on, and he grabbed my hand. I wanted to pull it away so he wouldn't be able to tell my entire body was shaking with the earthquake currently happening, but he held tight. He kissed my knuckles, and I noticed, from some far-off distance, that his lips were dry. His breath whispered across my skin. "If you want to go, I won't stop you. But we need to talk."

Those words again. His grip had loosened, and I tore my hand free. "No, we don't. I think it's clear what you're going to say. God, I can't believe I thought you were worth losing my family over."

Silence.

The door slammed behind me.

I hurried down the hall, not quite running, trying to get to the privacy of my car before the tears started falling. But I hoped this was one of those times when the love of my life would chase me down the hall and tell me it had all been a misunderstanding.

The door I'd left behind never opened.

As I cocooned myself in metal, my first tears fell.

CHAPTER SEVENTEEN

At home, the silence shouted my situation at me. I hadn't realized how used to another person's presence I'd become until it was suddenly gone with little hope of returning. The past week had just been a taste of what it was like now. Every movement made a resounding *boom* that echoed off the walls and bounded back into my chest. That was the only explanation for why I was shaking so hard, wasn't it?

I sank onto the couch, burrowing into the corner so that the back and arm embraced me, offering something stable to stop the world from rattling.

I'd lost Logan. But maybe I'd lost him long before this if he wasn't willing to move in with me. Maybe he'd been drifting farther and farther away, like two boats on the ocean, and it was only now that I'd turned to check that we were sailing in the same direction that I noticed he was lost over the horizon.

Oh fuck.

I clenched my hands in my shirt and smashed my lips against my knuckles. My breath sang like the whir of chopper blades over my fingers—*fuh fuh fuh fuh fuh*. My heart would have been beating just as fast if it hadn't given up altogether. I closed my eyes and forced in a deep breath. It rasped into me like shards of glass running down my chest, filling my lungs with their sparkling glitter.

Fuck. Fuck, I needed to get a hold of myself. This was . . .

Ridiculous? I didn't know. The only things holding me together were the threads of doubt that clung to my fragments, begging me to question if I had overreacted. But they were tenuous strings threatening to snap as my shaking continued. They weren't even strong enough to voice the concern as an actual thought—only a mere suggestion of the possibility that one day I'd look back and realize I'd done something foolish.

At the moment, everything I'd done felt foolish, so the suggestion that this, too, was foolish got lost in the quaking.

I wasn't sure how long I'd been sitting there, staring at the wall and the carpet and the backs of my eyelids. Long enough for darkness to settle over my apartment and a chill over my body. The shaking mellowed to quivers. Reality, or a sliver of reason, finally asserted itself:

I needed to talk to someone.

Who? A glance at my phone and my friends' thread reminded me that Jackson didn't want me around. So that cut Emmett out too. I swallowed, hard, and tucked myself deeper into the cushion. It was okay. It would be okay.

But I couldn't talk to Jenna, who would put on her counseling hat and psychoanalyze me—she'd tell me why I was being silly and make it all seem so clear-cut, like she always did. Maybe it was what I needed, but I couldn't handle that right now. Everything in her world was so . . . exact. And if I couldn't talk to her, I definitely couldn't talk to Laura, who'd either tell me to talk to Jenna or would blab everything to Jenna anyway.

Mark was terrible at this sort of thing and would likely run screaming into the metaphorical woods.

Roe. I really should have thought of them first. Roe was a good listener, and they offered input, not solutions.

I closed the group text and opened a text to Roe.

I took a deep breath, considered my words, then typed, *Hey, I need to talk. Call when you get a second.*

Send.

I stared at the screen. An inordinately long moment later, a check mark appeared by my text, telling me that they'd read it. I waited, my breath lodged in my throat. Waited for the icon to indicate that Roe was writing back or for the phone to switch to an incoming call. I waited until the screen went black, and then I waited a little more. I waited until the hum of activity in my neighbors' apartments went silent. As silent as my phone, which was as useful as a brick in my hand.

I waited forever. Then I turned off my phone, left it on the coffee table, and went to bed.

Without my phone alarm to wake me, it was purely the luck of insomnia that had me up and out of bed in time to go to work for the goddamned Saturday shift I'd offered to put in. Although, without having slept last night, I wasn't sure how much work I'd get done. I stood in the shower for fifteen minutes, ate a bagel without butter or cream cheese, remembered to put on clothes, and must have driven to work, because I was there swiping my card to enter the building.

Some of my coworkers were there, but none of us talked—we sat in our cubicles and focused on the tasks needed to complete the project. Our boss got us pizza for lunch. At two, everyone celebrated having finished the job and talked excitedly about what they planned to do with the rest of their weekend as they shut down their computers.

I listened to their chatter and let their joy wash over me, hoping I could ride the wave and find a hint of emotion besides exhausted numbness.

But the chatter about the weekend made me wonder if my friends' brunch was over and if they'd had fun. Sharp pain lanced my chest. I supposed it was better than the numbness.

On the drive home, I almost headed to Logan's house out of habit. When I jerked the wheel away from that exit, I nearly swerved into another car. A few tires squealed. Horns blared around me. I kept driving, staring ahead. Other than my stranglehold on the wheel, I was unaffected. My heart thumped along boringly. My head was blank but for the road stretched out in front of it.

Somehow I got home without causing any accidents.

In my cozy, echoing apartment, I changed into sweats and sat in front of the TV. For a moment I stared at the blank screen of my phone. Then I reached over, grabbed the remote, and turned the TV on. *The Big Bang Theory* covered the screen, and I set the remote down.

I didn't like this show, but I couldn't think of something I'd rather watch. At least now vibrant colors flashed across my vision. Voices and laughter filled my living room.

I pulled my knees up to my chest and wrapped my arms around my legs so I could rest my chin on my knees, getting comfortable as the commercials informed me this was a marathon running all weekend. Oh good.

Watching meant I didn't have to think about how my friends didn't want me. That Logan didn't want me. That all I had left was Sue. I hated that I'd been right. Sue was my family. The bonds to everyone else had snapped.

I should call Sue. I picked up the phone and waited for it to turn on, then impatiently clicked away from the various notifications, blaring bright on the screen. But once they were pushed aside, I saw the time. Nine o'clock on a Saturday wasn't a good time to call one's sister when she had a new boyfriend. I'd already driven everyone else away; I wouldn't want to piss her off too.

It could wait until tomorrow.

I blinked at the time again. Nine o'clock? Huh. I should probably eat dinner. I still had a packet of ramen in the cupboard.

CHAPTER EIGHTEEN

Morning came oddly early when you didn't sleep. It also lasted longer while I waited for a late enough hour to call my sister and not have her murder me.

When I finally deemed it a reasonable time, I skipped texting—my stomach lurching at the reminder of the unanswered one I'd sent to Roe—and called her.

"You're lucky I love you," Sue answered, humor in her tone. But she was right. "Good morning, Zacky."

"Morning," I croaked out. I blinked, stunned at my voice. It sounded weird. I cleared my throat and tried again. "Morning."

That was better. Less like a postmortem frog.

"You sick?" she asked. So maybe not as undead frog as I'd thought. I swallowed a gulp of coffee, which seemed to help. "No. I'm . . . not sick." Another swallow. "This isn't too early, is it?"

"Anything before noon on a Sunday is too early." Now her humor was starting to feel forced. "But nothing's too early for you, my dear brother."

There was a strange, sharp burning in my dry eyes and a tightness in my chest. Could insomnia cause a heart attack?

Then a warm trickle slid down my cheeks. Oh. I was weeping. Great.

"Isaac?" Her words were laced with concern. "You okay?"

"Um. No, not really." I paused, or maybe it was more of a hesitation, because I didn't want to confess how shit everything was at the moment, but she waited me out. She won, of course, because this was why I'd called. "My friends hate me, and I think Logan and I broke up."

It was definitely a pause on her end. "You think? You're not sure? What happened?"

So I told her about how Logan hadn't wanted to move in together until I told Mom and Dad, but that once I'd told them, he hadn't wanted to do it after all, and then what had happened on Friday night.

"Oh, Zacky," she said, voice full of sympathy. But it wasn't the sympathy I'd been expecting. Possibly pity rather than sympathy.

"What?"

"You say Logan wanted to talk to you. Why didn't you talk to him?"

"I didn't need to talk to him!" I might have shouted. "I knew what he was going to say! I didn't want to hear that."

She managed to make a sigh that sounded pitying *and* disappointed. She was a talented one, my sister. "How did you know what he was going to say?"

"Because he *wanted to talk*. That's what they always say. We need to talk and then we need to break up. I can read the signs! It doesn't take a genius when your long-term boyfriend doesn't want to move in together and then says you *need to talk*."

"Did he actually say he didn't want you to move in together?"

I opened my mouth to scream *yes*, but the word died in my throat. I licked my dry lips. "He wasn't very enthusiastic about it anytime I brought it up."

"Mm-hmm. Then he said he wanted to talk. Maybe he wanted to talk about why he 'wasn't very enthusiastic about it.'"

I answered her with silence. Partially because I was thinking about what she'd said. Partially because I was a stubborn ass sometimes, it seemed.

"Zacky, I love you, but . . ."

I knew she was only pausing to gather her words, yet I couldn't help squeaking, "But?"

"I love you. Never doubt that. But you know how you didn't want to tell Mom and Dad about being gay because you knew that conversation was going to hurt?"

I could have done without that reminder. "Yeah. And it did."

"I know. But you tend to avoid conversations that are awkward and possibly painful. I think maybe you're avoiding a conversation with Logan because it might hurt. And maybe it will. Maybe it won't. Sometimes the hurt is good."

"Good?" I scoffed. "Yeah, it was great losing Mom and Dad and getting *hit with a chair*."

"Sorry." I heard her wince. "Yes, the chair hurt and is shit and I still can't believe you didn't report him, but I'm not talking physical pain. I'm not trying to wave away losing Mom and Dad, either. But maybe it's healthier to lose them. Like . . . like when you have gangrene on a leg."

"What?"

Her chuckle trembled and sounded a little crazed. "Okay, go along with me here. So if your leg has gangrene, they might need to amputate. And it's shitty losing your leg. Yet if you don't lose your leg, you'll likely lose your life, so it's a good thing to lose your leg. Plus there are artificial legs you can get, and they're not quite the same, but they'll support you better than that horrible gangrene leg that would've killed you."

The metaphor was so gruesome and weird that I stopped and thought about it. Really thought about it. Eventually I said, "Did you just compare Mom and Dad to gangrene?"

"Yes!" she snapped. "Because they were toxic and slowly killing both of us. I'm glad you came out and they disowned you—er, sorry—but that happening gave me the strength to cut them out of my life too! And I feel so much better about myself and everything in my goddamn life now with them gone. Yes, it hurt to cut the limb off, but not having to fight that toxic shit anymore is going to make the rest of our lives so much better."

She was crying by the end of her speech, which was fitting since I was too.

It was several long minutes before we pulled ourselves together. Then I cleared my throat one more time. "I wish I was there to give you a hug."

She sniffled. "I'll get Dominic to give me one."

My wound that had sort of healed with our crying ripped back open. Logan wasn't here to give me a hug. He probably wouldn't want to. "Fuck."

In a strange moment of psychic ability, Sue said, "Go talk to him, Zacky. If he's going to break up with you—well, first off I'm going to rip his head off—"

"That's very praying mantis of you." I wasn't sure where the humor had come from, but it spilled from my mouth with an exhale.

"*Anyway*, if he is going to break up with you, it's better if you talk about it with him."

That's what a mature, responsible adult would do. Rather than run screaming from the apartment, saying they didn't think Logan had been worth coming out for.

Fuck. I'd said that, hadn't I? The night was a blur, but I recalled those words leaving my lips and hitting his face like a slap.

"Oh shit—" my voice hitched "—I'm an idiot, aren't I?"

"I think you've had a lot of shit go down," she said gently, "and you might have reacted poorly."

I hiccupped. "I love you."

"Love you too."

"I have to go."

"I know." The happiness in her voice curled around her words like a blanket. "Go get 'im, Zacky."

She hung up, but I stayed there, phone clenched in my hand.

"Go get 'im, Zacky."

As if it were that easy. As if I hadn't said something terrible enough to deserve to be dumped if he hadn't been planning to already. Oh god. What if he hadn't been planning to dump me and now he was? Oh fuck. Oh fuck, I'd messed this up. If only I'd stayed and—

Listened. Faced what he had to say, even if I didn't like it.

Oh.

A cold slime slunk down my back.

I should go talk to him. Clear the air.

Confront the consequences.

I hunched down over my phone, clenching my eyes closed as I hugged my knees and tried to breathe through the twelve-ton weight crushing my lungs. I'd said he wasn't worth it. I'd said the worst possible thing to him, the biggest fucking lie, and now he was going to dump me and I'd deserve it and . . .

And yet I needed to talk to him. If only to apologize for being a horrible boyfriend. A horrible person. Logan should *never* be told he wasn't worth it. Because he was.

He was even worth breaking my heart for all over again if I apologized and he still said goodbye.

Trembling, I stood.

The room spun around me, the colors smearing all over the place, and I clung to the back of the couch, as I waited for the spinning to stop and the colors to land where they belonged. I recalled the four cups of coffee I'd drunk and the ramen from the night before. My stomach was telling me it was hungry, but I didn't have time to give in to its whims. I'd grab something with another coffee from the drive-thru on the way to Logan's. I couldn't hesitate any longer.

I ran out the door, key and wallet in my hands.

The food helped clear my head and made me realize I probably shouldn't drink another coffee, based on how my heart was already racing. I also realized I was in the same sweats that I'd been wearing since about 3 p.m. yesterday and smelled faintly of BO. But as much as this wasn't the impression I wanted to give when having An Important Talk with Logan, I couldn't bear the thought of going home—to face the empty apartment and work up the nerve to leave again. So I went to Logan's.

He opened the door in sweats and with dark bags under his eyes. I briefly noticed that we were dressed to match, and then I said, "We need to talk."

I winced. I sounded exactly as he had a few days ago—like we were going to break up. He, on the other hand, didn't react. His face was all hard lines and a blank expression. He could be hiding anger or hurt, or both. I swallowed as he stepped back and gestured for me to enter.

A shiver passed through me as I walked past him, as if a chill radiated from him like an iceberg. My stomach lurched and tumbled, and I shoved my hands into my hoodie pocket and clamped them together, trying to stop the shaking from spreading.

"So what do you want?"

I spun to face him. He wasn't far from the entryway into the living room, as if he were a sentry, ready to kick me out. Oh fuck, he looked pissed.

I opened my mouth—

My jaw hung there, wet laundry on the line, airing all my embarrassing truths. Finally, finally, I managed to get the hinge working again. "I'm sorry."

His brow twitched, but otherwise his expression was unchanged. Unforgiving. "For what?"

Time to lay out my sins. My whole body shook as I dragged in a deep inhale. "For—for saying you weren't worth coming out for, because you are and it wasn't true in any way, shape, or form. It was a stupid thing to say anyway, because I didn't come out for you, I did it for me." My last bit of air squeaked out, and my body collapsed in on itself.

Logan crossed his arms over his chest, his biceps bulging, but it was his eyes that caught my attention. The stormy gray was clearing, and I could almost read his expression. "If you shouldn't have said it, then why did you?"

"Because I'm a goddamn idiot." I hesitated, then admitted, voice quiet, "Because I wanted to hurt you before you hurt me."

"Well, it worked," he said, voice flat. "You hurt me."

I flinched and hunched in on myself as tightly as I could. To be as small as I could. "I'm sorry."

He sighed, a giant exhale that blew the air from the room. I stayed motionless, waiting for . . . for what, I didn't know.

"You hurt me really bad, Isaac."

I dropped my eyes to the floor, then clenched them closed anyway. But I didn't run. I stayed to listen to what he had to say, although I was pretty sure I knew where it was going.

"I love you, and the fact you could say that, even during a fight, was . . . I didn't think you'd do that to me."

"You didn't deserve it," I said, so softly he might not have heard.

"I understand you were upset, but we needed to talk." He paused, and that moment lasted so long I almost died. Then he added, "We still need to talk."

I dared to unclench my eyes and peek up. He looked stern and serious as ever, but I saw now his arms were crossed *defensively*. Protecting himself from me. He thought he needed to . . .

My heart shattered. I swallowed the lump in my throat. "Yes. Let's talk."

"Can we start with what I wanted to say that night?"

I nodded and squeezed my own hand to keep from running.

"It wasn't that I didn't want to move in together. I did. But every time you brought it up, it reminded me that I'd hung it over your head like a noose. Or a prize."

I saw guilt on his face—the guilt I'd seen so many times before when I'd mentioned moving in—and suddenly it made sense.

"And because of that, you told your parents and they disowned you. It was all my fault. I never should have done that. I pushed you too hard—"

"No! No, I didn't come out to them for you. Or, rather, because of what you demanded. I won't lie that it was a bit of motivation, but I also can't blame you for that. While I had every right to wait until I was ready, you had every right not to be forced to take a step in the relationship that you didn't feel comfortable with." I inhaled sharply. The words that had spilled out seemed so logical. "And in the end, remember what we said in the car before we went into my parents' house? You said I didn't need to tell them. That we could move in anyway."

"I know, but—"

"And I said I wanted to tell them. I did. I don't regret it."

"But they—"

"I don't regret it," I repeated firmly, and took a step toward him, loosening my hands and letting them fall to my sides. "Losing them cut an unhealthy part out of my life. I have Sue and you—" I swallowed and *hoped* "—and my friends. You're—you're my family now."

Logan tilted his face up and met my gaze. "You're my family too. I should have talked to you earlier about what I was feeling. Before it all blew up."

"I should have too." I sighed. "I'm sorry I ran off. None of this would have happened if I hadn't."

"I should have done more to stop you. But then you said . . ."

"I'm sorry. I can't say that enough." Moving slowly, giving him time to step back if he didn't want me, I raised my hands and framed his face, meeting his eyes, hoping he looked into mine and knew how serious I was. "You are worth so much."

Because I was so very close, I saw his gaze soften with what I hoped was forgiveness. "Really?"

"Yes. I should never have said that, and I'm sorry. I was upset, and I will try so hard not to ever do something so hurtful again." I cleared my throat. "Sue says I maybe avoid difficult conversations."

Logan didn't say anything, only kept staring into my eyes.

"She might not have used the 'maybe,'" I confessed.

He chuckled, slid his arms around my waist, and began stroking my back. I rested my head against his shoulder so I could better sink my whole body against his.

"Are we okay?" I asked his neck as my tremors returned in earnest. Except it was in relief this time.

"Yes, I think we are. And I want you to move in with me. I'm excited about it, I swear. But I felt like such shit. Seeing you in the hospital, lost and confused. It was all my fault."

He sounded so broken. I wrapped my arms around him, hugging him and trying to hold him together. "It wasn't your fault. It was the fault of my homophobic asshole parents. I should have told them over the phone and then we never would have dealt with it. But I'm kinda glad I did it to their faces, because now I know for sure that I never want them in my life again."

His arms tentacled around me more tightly, keeping me as close as possible. "I love you."

I sighed, and all the tension seeped out of my body, leaving room for it to be infused with his warmth. It was heaven. I closed my eyes and smiled. "I love you too."

I wasn't even aware of falling asleep.

There were blankets over me, a soft mattress beneath me, and a hot body tangled around me. I smiled without opening my eyes.

"Welcome back, Sleeping Beauty."

I peeled my eyes open to his bedroom bathed in golden light. And his face close to mine, the amber glow highlighting all the sharp edges and strong lines. It must have been closer to lunch than dinner, and those three or four hours of sleep had been perfect. I would probably still crash hard tonight, but I no longer would be mistaken for a zombie. "Morning. Afternoon? Sorry about clocking out on you."

His lips quirked in a warm smile. "You needed it. I'm guessing you don't remember asking me to take you to bed or lose you forever?"

Heat rushed to my cheeks. "Um."

The smile rolled seamlessly into a chuckle. "I'm not certain you were awake for that."

"Uh, I plead, um, being in an altered state of mind?"

He wormed closer and kissed me. "That's not a thing."

"You stayed here with me?" I asked, totally not changing the topic.

"Of course." He grinned, that dangerous, playful one that I fell in love with every time I saw it. "I didn't want to lose you forever."

My stomach dropped out, free-falling as I considered how close we might have come. "No. No, wouldn't want that."

He must have heard something in the soft, choked whisper of my words, because he pulled me to him and threw a leg over my hips, tying me up with his limbs. But it was the absolute love in his eyes that really had me trapped there—not that I was even thinking of escaping.

I lurched forward to kiss him—because how could I not?—to let him know I felt the same way. It was only meant to be that, a kiss. But my forward motion rocked us, and he rolled onto his back, dragging me on top of him, our mouths still engaged. I gasped when his semihard cock pressed against my thigh. My own swelled in response. This was what he did to me.

"Are you still tired?" he asked against my lips.

Tired? When had I been tired? I was wide-awake now. A subtle adjustment of my hips pushed my cock against his through the thin layers of clothing that kept us apart. I was getting dizzy from the blood rushing to my dick so quickly. I groaned and thrust, only belatedly realizing that I hadn't yet answered him. "Not tired."

His laugh was a breathy whisper, more gasp than humor. "I see that."

It was my turn to throw him a grin that I hoped was sexy and not goofy. I *felt* sexy on top of him, a plan blooming in my mind. "But I could go for a bite to eat."

I dove under the sheets before he could think I was craving a sandwich, and tugged hard on the waist of his sweats. His cock bounced free as the material bunched on his thighs. Long and dark, exactly as I'd remembered it.

"No bites there," he protested, rather half-heartedly.

"Mmm, no, this is a full banquet." I let my breath tickle his cock as my lips traveled from base to tip. "Better start with an appetizer."

I licked the head, gathering up the hint of pre-come that had formed.

"Cannibal."

"Unrepentant." With that I sank my mouth down over him, taking him as fast and deep as I could.

A groan ripped out of him. "Fuck, Isaac!"

Any witty retort was stopped by his cock filling my mouth—probably for the best—so instead I enjoyed the slow slide off. I lathered him with my tongue, tasting every inch as he grew harder and larger.

It was a long, releasing sigh that spilled from his lips this time. I smiled when the cockhead popped free from my mouth, and I looked up at him, the miles of dark, tattooed skin between us. His answering smile was . . . happy. So goddamn happy. My heart swelled, and I sucked his cock in once again.

Like you did when you were overflowing with love for your super-hot boyfriend who you were going to move in with. Or at least that was my tactic.

At first I went slow, taking time to tease the head with my tongue, letting the air hit his spit-slathered skin. I stroked his balls with one hand while my mouth pumped his cock gradually to its fullness. At that point, Logan knotted his fingers in my hair.

"Please, Isaac, please."

I didn't make him tell me what he wanted so badly. And I didn't make him beg. Instead I sucked hard and fast, bobbing like my boyfriend's orgasm depended on it. The salty-sweet pre-come came faster, filling my mouth with his flavor. I had to let go of his balls to grab my own cock and ease the aching need there. It didn't take much: his grip tightening in my hair and forcing me down, just as I liked it, his come shooting down my throat.

A few more strokes to the music of his groans and I was coming too, making a mess of the sheets and struggling to breathe through the bliss. Maybe it was exhaustion or hunger or sheer relief, but my body kept shuddering with pleasure long after the last spurt. When I finally released him from my mouth and climbed up his body to collapse in a sated pile on top of him, he, too, was shaking with huge, gasping breaths.

We didn't speak. We clung to one another, sharing warmth and lazy come-flavored kisses until the trembling stopped. Then I sighed and sank against his chest as he dragged the blankets back over us.

"Isaac?" he murmured into the quiet that settled as securely as the blanket.

"Mmm?"

"Will you move in with me?"

I smiled, the rush of love swelling in my chest again. "I will."

CHAPTER NINETEEN

W e eventually made it out of bed and into the shower. By the time we finished there, we were ravenous, so we decided to order takeout. While he was on the phone, I checked mine, more from habit than any hope that people had reached out. The notification reminders still clung to the apps: three missed calls and one hundred fifty texts. One hundred and fifty. Most were in the group chat, but a few were only to me. The calls were Roe, Logan, and Emmett, although none had left messages—because in the age of texts, who needed to?

Speaking of, Roe had replied to my original text three hours after I'd sent it.

Sorry, didn't read your message until now, was in a movie. Wish I'd read it when it first came in :(Call me if you're still up and need to talk! Otherwise I'll call you in the morning <3

In a movie. A perfectly reasonable thing to do on a Friday night.

The messages in the group chat and in individual texts were all along the lines of *Isaac, you okay?*

In the group chat, I saw a bit more of the situation unfold. Saturday morning, Roe asking if anyone had heard from me. A flurry of concerns. Someone saying they'd ask Logan—at which point I wondered why I hadn't added him to that message string previously—and then they must have been together at brunch, because there was a series of *We're here if you need to talk* and *We love you* and *I'm breaking down your goddamn door on Monday if you're still MIA.*

Jenna should probably talk to Laura about her rather immediate inclination toward violence.

I stared at the texts from all of my friends, their voices of concern and love, and a smile crept brokenly across my face.

Logan joined me on the couch, sliding an arm around my shoulders. "Everything okay?"

I flashed him the screen—not nearly long enough for him to read it, because I had to look at the words again immediately. "My friends were worried about me."

"Sure they were; they're your friends."

"Yeah. Well." I swallowed, thinking about the last time I'd been with them. "I wasn't sure they'd still want me around. I said they were my friends, not my family. I hurt Jackson's feelings. I thought everyone low-key hated me for it. They . . . Fuck." I inhaled noisily. "Friday they made plans that they knew I couldn't make. I felt like they were cutting me off."

"Do you still think that?"

I shrugged, the pain from that night swelling up from where it had fallen forgotten under the crippling hurt of fighting with Logan. "Maybe. But I also think I need to talk to Jackson. Because I need to explain why I said that to him. To them. Maybe if they were cutting me out, it was because they didn't want me and Jackson to fight again."

"Or it was coincidence."

"Or that. Or maybe it was coincidence and Jackson was hurt and used it to lash out. Not, like, consciously. Heh." My laugh was flat and dead. "Maybe he was also avoiding a tough conversation."

Logan kissed my cheek. "If you need me to do anything, let me know."

I took a deep breath, then nodded. "If they're free tonight, will you go over with me to talk to Jackson?"

"Sure."

Because I wanted to delay the discussion with Jackson as much as possible, I hoped fate would intervene. Which meant when I texted Jackson, he said they were free and we could come over—which seemed to contradict what they'd said about Sunday being a bad day for brunch, but I tried not to jump to conclusions. Then the food arrived in the fastest show of delivery ever, and even eating seemed to take less time than usual.

Thankfully I had a change of clothes at Logan's place, which meant I was showered and in clean jeans and a hoodie when we went to Jackson and Emmett's place. It was unseasonably warm, so we bundled up and Logan drove me over on his bike. Maybe he wanted to take advantage of one last ride before conditions made it unpleasant. Maybe he knew that if this talk went badly, then a long trip on his bike, pressed close to him, the wind and noise cocooning me from the world, would be what I'd need. Or maybe he just wanted me snug against him after our own fight.

Riding on the back of his bike cleared my mind, shedding the tension and anxieties from earlier in the weekend, so when we pulled up to their house, I was almost ready to face Jackson as a reasonable adult. That didn't mean I wasn't scared shitless. Imagining life without all my friends—our weekends bullshitting and watching movies, the plethora of stupid links and images shared in chats, everything—hurt. Where would I even find new friends? I was too old to start over. And I liked the ones I had.

"Hey." Logan slipped his hand into mine and tugged me closer. "You okay?"

I startled and stared at him. He was smiling softly, as if maybe he'd said something and I'd missed it. "Sorry, thinking."

"They're your friends. You can talk this out."

"Yeah? But what if we keep fighting? Your friends seem to constantly be at each other's necks."

He shrugged, then dropped my hand to wrap his arm around my shoulders. "Well, first off, they aren't at the moment. But that's my point: they fight, and sometimes things are awkward, but eventually it works out. Secondly, I love my friends, but they do love their drama. Yours are much more low-key. I don't think you need to worry about this becoming a repeat performance."

I thought of my actions on Friday and how Jackson had left the room when we'd started arguing. No, my friends and I tended to avoid the drama—for better or worse. "I hope you're right."

Either way, I was learning that not having these conversations wasn't going to help anyone. My hand wasn't even shaking when I knocked on the door. But maybe that was more due to Logan's strong arm holding me close to him. Like my calm was from absorbing his strength rather than my own resolve.

Jackson answered the door in crisp jeans and a nice sweater—a bit overdressed for a Sunday afternoon. He smiled warmly, although a touch uncertainly, at both of us. "Hey, come on in."

We followed him into the living room, declining offers of drinks. Logan and I sat on the couch. I tried to relax. This was my old friend—nothing to be concerned about, right? No need to sit with my back ramrod straight, my hands clenched in my lap. And yet that was exactly how I sat. Jackson was my mirror image.

"Where are Rosa and Emmett?" I asked.

"Upstairs. Emmett wanted to give us some time to talk. Though he's possibly eavesdropping with a baby monitor; I wouldn't put it past him." Jackson tried for a smile.

I returned it just as weakly, my stomach lurching. Silence descended, but only for a moment.

"I'm sorry for what I said," I blurted.

Jackson blinked, face blank.

Heat rushed into my cheeks, and Logan reached over to break apart my hands and take one in his. I inhaled, shaking. "Sorry. I mean, I'm sorry for what I said the other day. When I said you weren't family. I—I don't think I explained myself very clearly. Or maybe I did and I was wrong. I don't know. But I don't want you to think that I think less of you guys because you're not my family." Logan squeezed my hand, and I added, "Not my biological family, I mean. That was your point, wasn't it? That I need to see family as more than blood."

I stumbled to a stop as Jackson started to nod. "Yeah." His Adam's apple bobbed. "It felt like we didn't mean as much to you as your family—who, no offense, treated you like shit. Um, aside from Sue."

"It's not like that." I hesitated, but another squeeze from Logan helped me continue. "See, there's nothing holding friends together. No twenty or thirty years of shared history. No childhoods. No spending every waking moment together and holidays and all that. So friends, when they fight, it's easy for them to break apart. To stop hanging out. To vanish from each other's lives. But family is obligated to love you—" I winced and closed my eyes as a sharp pain shot through my chest.

A second later the cushion on the other side of me sagged, and Jackson's arms wrapped around me. I opened my eyes, a little stunned. The hug didn't last long, but he kept one arm across my shoulders.

"To me," Jackson said softly, "family isn't those people who love you because they're obligated; it's the people who love you because they love you. The people who love you because they're obligated are relatives—linked by blood, but not much else. People who love you because they love you—that's family. Sue is a relative and family. But I think of you as my family, Isaac."

"Yeah." My voice cracked, and I had to swallow twice. "That's a good point."

"I guess we both didn't explain ourselves very well the other day."

"So, we're okay now? I can't promise this whole 'my friends are my family' thing is going to be automatic, but you guys mean the world to me. Is that enough?"

Jackson nodded. "We're okay. And I'll be patient. Emmett and Roe had a talk with me about expecting everyone to immediately fall in line with my worldview."

I chuckled at the image of the two of them ganging up on Jackson. Knowing how stubborn Jackson could be, it would probably take two of them to do it. "So, I'm forgiven?"

"Yes!" He pulled me into a tight hug again, and it might have been to hide his tears, because his voice was a little choked when he added, "That's what family does."

I planned to blame my own tears on my utter exhaustion. Thankfully there was no one here who needed to be given the excuse.

Eventually the hug ended, and we wiped our faces and took deep breaths.

My chest was still tight. "There's one more thing."

"Go on." His eyes were wide, maybe with a bit of terror.

"Friday night, when you planned the brunch. I couldn't do Saturday and you said it was the better day, but you . . . I mean, you're not . . ." I grimaced. "Did you do that so I wouldn't be there?"

If possible, his eyes got wider. "No! Hell, Isaac, no." He exhaled sharply. "I won't deny I was still pretty pissed at you. But we were supposed to have a gathering at noon today with Emmett's extended family—relatives, so a brunch would have been rushed. Then they all fucking bailed at the last minute." His jaw clenched, as if holding back curses he wanted to lay on said relatives. When it relaxed, he said, "I'm sorry. My feelings probably meant I wasn't being fair to you. I'm sorry for the brush-off." A smile peeked through. "If it helps, we spent the whole time talking about you."

I bumped his shoulder with mine. "Liar. I bet half the time was talking about Rosa and that new show."

He laughed. "You got me." A pause. "Hey, um, I know it's last minute, but I could invite everyone over for an early dinner. Since you didn't get to hang out with us this weekend."

I glanced to Logan, who was watching us with the dopiest smile. He didn't even need to nod for me to know he was up for it. I turned back to Jackson. "Sounds good."

The perk of Emmett eavesdropping through the baby monitor—aside from the fact that Jackson and I got to tease him about it—was that we didn't need to explain or talk about everything that had happened.

The same could not be said for the rest of our friends.

Roe was the first to arrive, which was a pleasant surprise because, despite living the closest, they hated last-minute plans. I opened the door, and they nearly tackled me to the floor with a hug. A string of "Oh my god I'm sorry I wish I'd gotten the message sooner and I'm glad you're okay and I was worried and I love you, you know that don't you?" all escaped in one impressive breath.

"I love you too." The heat of my blush flared up my neck. I shouldn't be embarrassed about saying those words to my friends, but it wasn't something I was used to doing. I promised to change that. "C'mon in. Jackson and I talked. Logan and I talked. All is okay."

Roe clung to my arm a bit as we headed to the living room. Their voice was low and quiet, as if for my ears only. "I was worried about you. I thought . . . But I didn't know what to do if you had."

I scrunched my brow. "You thought what?"

Roe glanced up and then away. "Nothing. You didn't, so it's okay."

We hadn't gotten to the room with everyone else, so I stopped us and turned Roe to face me. My heart was fluttering like I'd had too much coffee. I was having so many conversations this weekend that I would have rather not. "It *is* okay. But if you need to talk to me about it, I'm here. You know?"

They met my gaze, a smile tugging at the corners of their mouth. "And I'm here if you need me. Even if I don't reply immediately—God, I wish I'd read your text before the movie." They huffed, seemingly in frustration with themself, then stared, steely-eyed at me. "Don't cut us off like that. Please?"

I nodded, hoping the urge would never again come up quite so intensely as it had this weekend. "I promise. I just didn't want to hear that you didn't want to talk to me." Admitting it had the blush flooding warmth up to my cheeks.

They only burned hotter when Roe hugged me for a second time. "Never!"

Logan's chuckle broke us apart. "Roe, you're going to kill my boyfriend with embarrassment."

Roe, who didn't look embarrassed or called out in the least, beamed at Logan. "I wanted him to know I care."

Without their gaze on me, I was able to say, "I know that now."

I went through similar conversations with my other friends as they showed up, although none were quite so intense as that first one with Roe. When everyone had arrived, we sat around the kitchen table, sharing the roast chicken dinner and the various other food items people had brought, laughing, talking, and generally being exactly as we always were.

Just like a family.

EPILOGUE

"**H**ot stuff coming through!" I announced, carrying the steaming sweet-potato casserole out to the improvised dining room table we'd set up.

"And he brought the potatoes too," Logan said behind me, the turkey platter in hand.

"Aren't you funny." I resisted rolling my eyes as I set the casserole on the pot holder, but my cheeks were burning with a smile and embarrassment.

"I told you they were making out in the kitchen," Jenna said.

Laura rolled her eyes. "Ugh, newlyweds."

I stepped back and raised an eyebrow at her. "We're not married."

"You're living together—that's practically the same thing."

"So you and Jenna are celebrating your, what, fifth wedding anniversary this year?"

She picked up a roll as if to throw it at me, and I scuttled back to the kitchen to fetch the cranberry sauce. By the time I returned and took my seat next to Logan, everything was out and people were seated, sipping their wine and waiting to dig in. Thankfully conversation had moved on from what Logan and I had—or had not—been up to in the kitchen.

"Before we begin, I'd like to say a few words," Logan said, standing, eliciting playful groans from our friends. He cleared his throat and passed a glare around. "As I was saying. I want to thank everyone for joining Isaac and me for our first Christmas together."

A collective "Awww" rang out, and despite the fact I knew they'd done it on purpose, my cheeks heated again. I wanted to duck my head, but I kept my eyes locked on Logan.

"It means a lot to us that we can gather here together with the people we love, who support us—"

"And heckle us," I chimed in.

Logan grinned and rested his hand on my shoulder, giving it a firm squeeze. "And put up with us and our dramatics throughout the year."

"And thank you for putting up with our dramatics too, Isaac!" Erika said.

Logan sighed. "Am I going to be able to get through this speech? Do you *want* to eat?"

A chorus responded:

"Oh, like you want all these leftovers."

"Friends don't threaten friends!"

"I'm starving!"

"Speech! Speech! Speech!"

"*As I was saying*," Logan continued, silencing the racket. "With the wonderful, and sometimes difficult, year Isaac and I have had, we appreciate you standing by us and being our family."

I tensed and swallowed the lump in my throat. Logan squeezed my shoulder again. I wasn't actually missing Mom and Dad, who I'd heard nothing from in the past month. Not that I was expecting to. Good riddance, as Sue said. Her, I was missing. She'd decided to spend this Christmas with her boyfriend and his family—yes, that was moving fast—but she'd been over the night before to celebrate Christmas Eve with us. Logan and her boyfriend got along in that way that made significant others roll their eyes.

"We're both grateful for everything you guys have done for us, whether it's listening, loving, or smacking sense into us. Thank you," Logan finished, his voice a little choked.

"Cheers!" Jenna said, raising her glass.

"Cheers!" everyone echoed, including Logan and me. The room filled with the *clink* of wineglasses.

"And with that," Logan said, sitting back down, "let's eat!"

When he was within reach, I gripped his hand tightly, leaned over, and kissed his cheek, my eyes burning and my throat tight. "Merry Christmas."

He turned his head, his own eyes suspiciously shiny. "Merry Christmas."

Then he kissed me, the smile on his lips matching the one on mine.

Dear Reader,

Thank you for reading Alex Whitehall's *Hard Truths*!

We know your time is precious and you have many, many entertainment options, so it means a lot that you've chosen to spend your time reading. We really hope you enjoyed it.

We'd be honored if you'd consider posting a review—good or bad—on sites like **Amazon, Barnes & Noble, Kobo, Goodreads, Twitter, Facebook**, **Tumblr,** and your blog or website. We'd also be honored if you told your friends and family about this book. Word of mouth is a book's lifeblood!

For more information on upcoming releases, author interviews, blog tours, contests, giveaways, and more, please sign up for our weekly, spam-free newsletter and visit us around the web:

> **Newsletter**: riptidepublishing.com/newsletter
> **Twitter**: twitter.com/RiptideBooks
> **Facebook**: facebook.com/RiptidePublishing
> **Goodreads**: tinyurl.com/RiptideOnGoodreads
> **Tumblr**: riptidepublishing.tumblr.com

Thank you so much for Reading the Rainbow!

RiptidePublishing.com

ACKNOWLEDGMENTS

A big shout-out to my betas and sensitivity reader for all your insight and advice; to Caz for cleaning up all my many, many crutch words; and to L.C. for making my vague cover idea come to life. Also, I couldn't have done this without the support of my own chosen family and my own biological one: I got lucky twice.

ALSO BY
ALEX WHITEHALL

Magic Runs Deep
Second Skin
Sharing a Pond
A Christmas for Oscar
As the Snow Falls

ABOUT THE AUTHOR

If there are two types of people in the world, Alex Whitehall probably isn't one of them, despite being a person. Their favorite pastimes include reading, horseback riding, sleeping, watching geek-tastic television, knitting, eating, and running. And wasting time on the internet. And spending glorious evenings laughing with friends.

While Alex prefers sleeping over doing anything else (except maybe eating), sometimes they emerge from the cave to be social and to hunt for food at the local market. They can be found blogging, reading, and tending after their aloe plants.

Connect with Alex:

Twitter: @AlexWhitehall

Email: AlexDWhitehall@gmail.com

Blogging: alexwhitehall.blogspot.com

Tumblr: alexwhitehall.tumblr.com

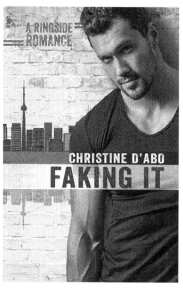
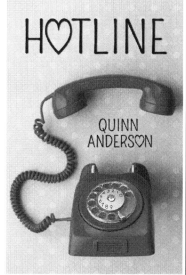